Workers Write!

More Tales from the Classroom

Edited by David and Robin LaBounty

Blue Cubicle Press

Published by
BLUE CUBICLE PRESS, LLC
Post Office Box 250382
Plano, Texas 75025-0382

ISSN 1556-715X
ISBN 978-1-938583-22-3

Printed in the United States of America

Introduction by Robin LaBounty. Copyright © 2019 by Blue Cubicle Press, LLC.

Credits:

"Abdicated" by Linda Sánchez first appeared in the Summer 2007 (9.2) issue of
    The First Line.
"Untethered" by Lisa Heidle first appeared in the Winter 2010 (12.4) issue of
    The First Line.
"The Great White Way Is Where the Heart Is" by Isabella David first appeared in
    the Winter 2012 (14.4) issue of *The First Line*.
"Fast Classroom Exit" by Sarah Bigham first appeared in Issue XLII of *Roanoke
    Review*.
"The Classroom" by Sarah Bigham first appeared in Issue 13 of *The New
    Southern Fugitives*.
"Not By Arguments" by Tony Press first appeared in the March 2017 issue of
    Gravel.
"In Bloom" by Allie Marini first appeared in the Summer 2012 (14.2) issue of
    The First Line.

Contents

Introduction

We published the predecessor to this collection of stories, *Tales from the Classroom*, in 2006. Although it's only been thirteen years, the teaching profession has endured many changes, both positive and negative, and yet teachers remain one of the most influential cornerstones of our communities. The stories collected here hopefully reflect this.

A.J. Howells story, "Dropping Out," reminds us that no matter how schools and students change there will always be reluctant minds to nurture, and sometimes you win the battle but lose the war. Sheryl Guterl's, Victoria Crawford's, and John Jeffire's poetry show us that there are new, complicated obstacles that students and teachers have to overcome. Several of the stories are honest reminders of educators who, even though they try to do what they think is best, end up failing and have to accept the consequences and move on.

My own experiences with the world of education have shifted recently. After fifteen years of being a parent and a substitute, my children are now in college, and I have a full-time job in a high school library. It is a different view, but I've noticed the players are the same. Students who are on their journey to figuring out learning, relationships, and their place in the world will always need teachers there to guide the way. I am thankful for the teachers who made me who I am, a person who can go forward and hopefully give the same back to my students. And I am happy to have these stories of other like-minded educators to keep me company.

Robin

Ode to a Noisy Faculty Room

The faculty room is where I go
without much fanfare,
to get off my feet and a bite to eat.

When I take my seat
among friends and I-don't-knows,
the show begins with talk of kids and salads.

Some crow about sports, kids, pets, or trips.
Some dream about cruises or new kitchens.
Some praise kids, parents, politicians, schools, and society.
Some blame kids, parents, politicians, schools, and society.
Some sing a quiet tune.

Some talk of happy things—promotions,
presents, parties, births, weddings, showers,
movies, retirement, and more.

Some talk of sad things—unemployment,
drugs, divorces, diseases, cancer, dying,
movies, death, and more.

Nobody has it made in this passing parade,
but when I walk out I know there's hope
because we're all in the same boat
and somehow we'll stay afloat.

—*Joe Sottile*

Room 217

Barb Miller

Janice Harvey checked her lipstick in the rear-view mirror and wiped the excess from her front teeth. Though she missed teaching, she'd taken her time getting on the district's substitute list. Her husband's job promotion required leaving Oregon in 1974 and moving to a small town in McCurtain County, Oklahoma, which consisted of three stores and a post office. She left her two-story house and the support of her family to embrace life in a single-wide mobile home, Weyerhaeuser's relocation housing perk for their employees. Janice had her hands full with two children in grade school and a two-year-old, but her husband insinuated she was wasting her education staying at home. When the school secretary called, she offered Janice a weeklong assignment with a half day on Monday. Miss Conrad's learning disabled class had only seven students. Janice wavered. She loved the intimacy of individualized instruction. Also, Janice's childless neighbor, who made herself a household fixture, overheard the conversation and offered to babysit. So, she accepted.

Janice arrived Monday, mid-morning, and waited in the K-8 school office for Mr. Davies, the principal. Around 10:30, he emerged from his office, greeted her, and steered her out the double doors to the playground. A teacher was positioned on the steps, wielding a hack paddle.

"I have to go to the toilet," whined a six-year-old.

"Nope. Shoulda gone before ya came out," warned the teacher, slapping the paddle against her thigh. Janice was taken aback. Physical punishment in Oregon schools was outlawed years ago.

They crossed the playground and entered a flat-roofed,

disfigured, stucco building that appeared vacant. As they traveled down the long hall, Janice noticed the rooms were a boneyard for classroom furniture and antiquated textbooks.

"Miss Conrad's lab is equipped with remedial reading and math resources for kids who are learning disabled. The students listen to individualized lessons on headphones and she monitors their progress. Are you familiar with the equipment?"

"Somewhat. If I have a question, I'm sure the students will share their technical expertise." She smiled.

The principal raised an eyebrow. "The equipment is expensive. If you need help, send a kid for Mr. Floyd, the janitor."

Room 217 was labeled *LD* in black letters on the doorframe. Shouting echoed from inside and shadows darted across the green window glass on the upper half of the door. The voices stopped abruptly, as Mr. Davies turned the knob and opened to a wall of warm stale air and five students sitting in wooden flip-top desks. Janice smiled, but only one child made eye contact. The smallest boy slumped over his desk with his head on his arms. A much older boy stared out the window. The two girls studied her in quick glances, looking away when she tried to catch their eye. She surveyed the room. The high ceiling was plated in metal tiles and exuded streaks of rust down the dirty stucco walls. The floor was tiled in green linoleum squares, and a mop bucket leaned against a utility sink in one corner. Yellowed sunbaked blinds covered most of the tall windows, hanging haphazardly at different levels. The actual remedial lab consisted of three plywood cubicles in the middle of the room, each with a desktop and chair. A tangle of cables careened out from under each nook and connected to a wad of extension cords, which traveled under several empty desks to a coverless outlet. A collage of colored gum wads coated the inside of the last cubicle. Janice felt overdressed in her beige suit and heels.

"Mornin', class," said Mr. Davies, looking surprised. "Miss Conrad left already?"

"Yes, sir," a boy nodded.

"Where are the Shuler twins?" asked Davies.

"They got head lice," said the boy, rolling his dark brown eyes and scratching his head. "Stay away from there, Mr. D." He pointed to the desk next to where the principal was standing.

"Well then," said Davies, moving away. "This is Mrs. Harvey. She's fillin' in for Miss Conrad this week." A girl with bleach-streaked hair smirked and forced her tongue through a wad of purple gum.

"Miss C got cooties?" asked the girl, snickering.

"No, Lou Anne. She's at a workshop," said Davies, moving toward the teacher's desk. "Here's her lesson plans, Mrs. Harvey. Lunch is from noon to one. The kitchen sends the kids' trays over on a cart. You're welcome to eat in the teachers' lounge."

"Thanks," said Janice, realizing she forgot to pack a lunch.

"Y'all help Mrs. Harvey. Ya hear?" said Davies, pulling the door shut behind him.

"She's gone a lot," said James. "She tell you 'bout the checks? If somebody's bad, she puts their name on the chalkboard an' a check. Three checks an' you get hacked. I don't ever, but Hobo gets it a bunch." He pointed to the small boy bent over his desk. "Your name's Harley, like a

Harley hog?" he asked, grinning. The older boy snorted.

"It's Harvey, Mrs. Harvey, and yours is...?"

"James Cooper Benton. Know my facts to the sevens, and I'm the best reader." He lowered his voice. "These guys are dumber 'n doornails."

"Shut up, James!" snapped Lou Anne. "You got diarrhea of the mouth." Everyone laughed, except the other girl in the back row with dark circles under her eyes.

"That's enough," warned Janice, thumbing through the papers. "What are you working on right now?"

"Word search," said James, "an' I'm always done first."

"That's 'cause you cheat off mine," said Lou Anne, waving hers in the air.

"Liar!" yelled James. He left his desk and slid into one in front of the small boy. "Wake up, Hobo!" he said, smacking the boy's desktop.

Janice printed *Mrs. Harvey* and the date on the chalkboard. "I need to learn your names," she said, moving toward them. "You're James and you're Lou Anne. Right?"

The girl with the dark circles lifted her hand. "I'm Shelly," she said, peering out through straight black bangs. She slumped over her desk with her arms crossed, as if shielding her body.

"I have a niece named Shelly," said Janice, touching the girl's shoulder. Shelly winced and pulled away.

"She can't read worth beans," blurted James. "Miss C lets her clean the chalkboards."

"Shut up, James!" shot Lou Anne.

"*Please*, raise your hand if you have something to say." Janice moved to the small boy. "And you are...?"

James pulled the boy's arm toward him, revealing the open

blade of a pocketknife in his hand. "Uh, oh. Not s'posed to have knives at school. Get expelled! He gets a check for that!"

"You ain't the teacher," sneered Lou Anne.

"That's enough!" warned Janice. "Your name is Hobo?" she asked, leaning in.

"Yes, ma'am." He grinned sheepishly, exposing several decayed teeth.

"Please close the knife and give it to me," she said, extending her hand.

Hobo closed it, but slid his arm away from her, revealing deep cuts in the desktop.

"What have you done to your desk?" she exclaimed. Hobo spread his arms over the gouges.

"Miss C gonna be pissed!" blurted James.

"Let's have it," she demanded. Hobo shook his head side to side.

James grabbed the knife. "Here, teacher," he said, handing it to her. Hobo jumped out of his seat and crashed his way to an empty desk near the door. "Ain't sittin' by no snitch," he muttered.

Janice put the knife in the desk drawer and wrote Hobo's name with a check on the chalkboard. "Now," she said, breathing deeply as she moved toward the last student who appeared to be much older, maybe thirteen. He was twice the size of the other boys, with a barrel chest, dark skin, and a shock of black straight hair. "Would you share your name?"

"He's Choctaw an' he don't talk," said James.

"Quit flappin' your gums," said Lou Anne.

"That's enough, Lou Anne." Janice moved to the chalkboard and wrote her name with a check. "What do you mean he doesn't talk?" she asked James.

"Not to Miss C, he don't." James shrugged.

"His name's Chip," said Shelly. "He's my cousin." The boy glanced at her and then stared straight ahead. "His mom cooks at the Quail Cafe." Chip pulled his lips together, trapping a smile.

"I've eaten there," said Janice. "Your mom's a cook, Chip?" she asked, prompting him.

"He ain't gonna talk, lady," said Hobo.

Lou Anne got up and sidled up to Janice. "I need a pad," she mumbled. Her breath was sour, and dirt lines trailed around her arms and neck. A filthy bra strap hung below one shirtsleeve.

"I'm sorry, I didn't hear—"

"I need a pad," said Lou Anne, exaggerating the 'p.' "Miss C puts 'em in that drawer."

"Oh, sorry," she stammered. The room grew silent as they approached the desk. Janice discreetly handed her a Kotex.

"Whatcha starin' at, people?" Lou Anne shrieked, waving the blue box in the air. She slammed the classroom door behind her. James and Hobo hooted. Janice felt her cheeks flush.

"Hobo?" Janice pointed to the door. "We need to talk."

"Damn!" He got up reluctantly, shoving the desks on his way to the door.

"Ooh. Bad boy! Not s'posed to cuss!" blurted James.

"Bastard," Hobo sneered.

Janice added checks under both boys' names and joined Hobo in the hall. She told him that he was destroying his folks' property when he cut his desk. Did he know that their taxes pay for everything at school? "And swearing is rude,

Hobo. Your bad attitude and language offend everyone, not just James. I'm sure Mr. Davies and Miss Conrad would be disappointed with your behavior today."

"They don't give a crap! And my folks don't pay no taxes, 'cause they get a govament check. And James *is* a bastard 'cause he ain't got no daddy. He flat told me that."

Janice smelled cigarette smoke and instantly connected it to Lou Anne in the restroom. Before she could address that issue, the bell clanged from inside the room, and three of the children pressed up against the door. A kitchen worker jockeyed a cafeteria cart through the front entrance of the building. Was it noon already? Janice opened the classroom door slowly and blocked the entrance with outstretched arms.

"Gotta wash up," James protested. "That's what we do."

"No, this is what we do. Return to your desks. When you're quiet, I'll excuse you one at a time."

"Stupid!" said Hobo.

"You'll be last, Hobo. Sit down!" She dismissed each one and escorted Hobo down the hall. A thick fog filled the girl's restroom. The girl sat on the edge of the sink, smoking.

"Give me the cigarettes, Lou Anne."

"Empty," she quipped. She wadded up the Marlboro pack and dropped it on the floor. "It's no big deal. Miss C. smokes in here, too, but she don't know I seen her." She inhaled deeply, blew the smoke upward, and snuffed the butt in the sink.

"Out! Now!" said Janice. Lou Anne slid off the sink and sauntered into the hall.

When Janice returned to the classroom, the boys had already crammed their half-eaten trays onto the cart and bolted for recess. Lou Anne refused to eat 'that crap' and went outside. Shelly begged to stay in the room.

"You can't, Shelly. I'm locking up, but I'll wait until your done eating."

"Not hungry," she said, putting her untouched tray back on the cart. When Janice went inside the room, Shelly headed toward the restroom.

Surely the afternoon would be more productive. The heat in the room was oppressive. Janice peeled off her jacket, added a check to Lou Anne's name, and tried to open a window. It wouldn't budge. She tried another to no avail. Frustrated, she locked the door and hurried over to the office, wracking her brain for an afternoon activity that might provide positive reinforcement and get them back on schedule. They definitely needed stiff consequences for their misbehavior, but it wouldn't be hacking, at least not on her watch. She rarely spanked her own kids. Cooling the room down would improve everyone's attitude, hers included. She asked for Mr. Davies in the office but was told he'd also gone to the workshop. After inquiring about art supplies, the secretary directed her to the art room, where a woman her age was hanging wet finger paintings. Janice introduced herself and shared the behavior incidents and the overheated room.

"If I use an art activity as a reward, we might actually get some work done," Janice confided.

"Ever done clay?" asked the woman.

"Does eight years of Play-Dough count?" They both laughed. "Actually, I made a slab box and a pinch pot in college."

"That'll work. I have a twenty-five-pound block of natural

clay that's still good. My kiln died. You're welcome to it, but it's dark brown and messy," she warned.

"Can't hurt *that* room," said Janice, matter-of-factly.

"I have to admit, I've been here for nine years, and I've never been in that building."

"You're not missin' much. Mr. Davies seems pretty familiar with the room, though."

The art teacher snickered. "He and Conrad have a thing goin'." She hoisted the bagged clay from a bottom shelf. "Here you go. There's a slicing wire and a few wooden tools in the bag. Hope it works out. Sorry, I missed your name."

"Janice Harvey, and yours?"

"Becky Nelson. I could use a sick day and I'll need a good sub." She smiled.

A janitor rounded the corner and jockeyed his keys into a hallway door.

"Excuse me," said Janice.

"Yes, ma'am?"

"Are you Mr. Floyd?"

"Yes, ma'am. You need somethin'?"

"Yes. I'm subbing in the LD room. It's so hot. I can't get the windows open."

"Them windows are painted shut, ma'am. Can't remember when they wasn't. I can scrounge up a fan or two if that'll help."

"That would be great."

"I'll be over directly. I'm fixin' to clean up puke in the lunchroom."

Janice felt sweat run down the inside of her shirt as she crossed the wall of playground noise. The sun was straight overhead and the humidity extreme. As she put the key in the door, she heard the sound of running water coming from the end of the hall. She propped the clay against the door and headed that way. Water pooled at the entrance to the boys' restroom. She called out, and when no one answered, she leaned in. Both faucets were running, and the sinks were stuffed with paper towels. Water spilled onto the floor toward the drain which was clogged with toweling as well, forcing water into the front stalls. Janice removed her wet heels and waded in to shut off the water, gagging at the smell of urine as she clawed paper from the sink drain. When she finished, she went into the girls' restroom to wash up and noticed feet on the floor of the last stall.

"Who's in here?" she asked, snapping paper towels from the dispenser. Shelly emerged from the stall, wide-eyed and nervous.

"Shelly, have you been here the whole time?"

"I felt sick," she answered.

"Did you see who made this filthy mess?"

"No," said Shelly, averting her eyes. Janice grabbed two rolls of towels from the top of the dispenser and handed them to the girl.

"Can you carry these, please?" she asked, clutching a wet shoe in each hand. Janice unlocked the classroom, set her heels inside, and dragged the clay into the room.

"What's that?" Shelly asked pointing to the bag.

"Clay. I thought we might do an art project this afternoon, but now, I'm not so sure."

"That's why I hate this class! Whenever somebody does somethin' bad, we all get punished." She started crying.

Janice stuffed paper into her shoes. "You're not in trouble, Shelly," she said, handing her a tissue. "We do need to cover the desks with paper towels. Would you cut some?"

"Okay," she sniffed.

"When you finish, I'll show you how to slice natural clay with a wire. It's like slicing cheese." Janice was pounding on another window frame when the janitor arrived, carrying a fan in each hand.

"You ain't kiddin' 'bout the heat, ma'am. Could fry an egg in here. Wastin' your time on them windows." He plugged both fans into the wall. "Leastways, it'll blow some air around."

"Thank you, Mr. Floyd. Before you go, can you check the boys' restroom? Someone plugged the sinks and the floor drain during lunch. There's still a lot of water on the floor."

"As if I ain't got enough to do! They pull that stunt every time there's a sub, which is a lot. You find out who's doin' it, you better tan their hide. They're gettin' away with murder." The bell went off and within minutes, the other students burst into the room, bantering noisily, until they saw the janitor.

"Which one of you boys pranked the john?" he barked. He needn't have asked. Hobo's pants were water-stained from his knees to his shoes.

"Now we gonna have to use the girls'!" said James, grinning.

"Don't worry, Mr. Floyd," said Janice. "I'll get to the bottom of this." James wagged his hand in the air, but she ignored him. When a blast of hot air from the rotating fan hit her in the face, she decided to forget the lab. She'd just do the clay, try to get better acquainted, and survive the afternoon. She'd make up the lab time tomorrow.

"Wash your hands back at the sink and take your seats.

Since it's so hot, we're going to have an art lesson. Shelly will give you each a slice of clay. You can start by rolling it into a ball. We'll make clay pots and decorate them with Indian symbols. Who knows? Maybe Chip and Shelly know some Choctaw designs. Hobo, I need to talk to you in the hall."

"Again? Why you only pick on me?"

"I knew he did it!" James blurted. "Don't send him to the office! He'll run off."

"James, zip your lip!" she said sternly, pointing to the chalkboard and ushering Hobo out the door. Lou Anne hooted.

"Hobo, did you make that mess in the bathroom?" she asked. He set his jaw and stared at the floor.

"Am I gettin' a check?"

"Did you?" she demanded. He cocked his head to the side and rolled his eyes.

She felt the tension in her shoulders and realized that her jaw was clenched. She was so fed up with this game. It seemed he was purposely misbehaving to get punished. James was right; he'd never make it to the office. If she sat him in the hall, he might destroy something else. She had no choice but to keep him in the room, monitor the others, and write it all up later. Mr. Davies could deal with him tomorrow, or whoever. She didn't care as long as they kept him there. She grabbed the doorknob.

"Go to your seat and get out paper and a pencil. You'll write an apology to Miss Conrad and Mr. Davies, telling them that you flooded the restroom during lunch, cut holes in your desk, and used swear words in class. You'll also write a note to Mr. Floyd to apologize for the mess you made. I'll take your letters over with my report after school. Tomorrow morning, go straight to Mr. Davies's office.

"I'm gettin' a check, right?" Frustration gripped every nerve in her body. She leaned forward, locking eyes with him.

"Get started! Now!"

"Bitch," he mumbled.

She closed the door forcefully, rattling the glass. Shelly had flattened her clay into a pancake and was carving her initials. Chip was rolling a thick log. Lou Anne and James had scooted together and were squeezing the clay from their hands into piles of poop, laughing hysterically. Janice strode to the chalkboard and added a check below three names: Lou Anne, James, and Hobo. The talking stopped, but the chanting began.

"Hack! Hack! Hack!" Even Chip mouthed the words. "Hack! Hack! Hack!"

"Stop right now!" said Janice forcefully.

"Hobo's gotta get hacked. Three checks and you get hacked," said James, pointing to the chalkboard.

She glanced at Hobo, but he was grinning at Chip, who'd turned his log into a male body part.

"Chip made a pecker," he hooted. Everyone howled. Chip's name went on the board, and they chanted again.

"Hack! Hack! Hack!" Hobo stood and did a few dance moves.

Janice walked over and turned off the lights. "Put your heads down on your desk! Everyone!" She was amazed when they actually responded. She glanced up at the clock. In less than an hour, they'd be gone, but she'd have to face them in the morning...and the rest of the week. The day was wasted and she had aided and abetted the inmates. There was nothing to do but clean up, lock up, and start fresh in the morning with expectations and a schedule. Janice sat at the desk and jotted notes in the planner. Forty minutes later, she flipped on the lights.

"Roll your clay into a ball and return it to Shelly. Wipe off your desk and put the paper towels in the trash. I better not see any clay on the floor." Suddenly, something hit the side of her head. Then a brown splotch appeared on the front of her shirt. Clay balls were sailing across the room from every direction.

"Stop it! All of you!" she shrieked, but it takes time to stop a train.

"Hey!" said James, pointing to the clock. "We gotta clean up. Hobo's gettin' hacked." Janice watched in disbelief as they piled the clay on Shelly's desk, wiped their desks, and retrieved a fair amount of clay balls from the floor. Within five minutes of the bell, their sweaty bodies enveloped Hobo and moved like an amoeba toward her desk. The boy doubled over in front of her.

"Your underwear's showin'," sang Lou Anne.

"Pervert!" quipped James, pulling Hobo's shirt down.

"Hack! Hack! Hack!" they chanted.

Janice felt nauseated, and the slight pain above her eye had become a pounding headache. This was pointless. Hacking wouldn't fix any of them. The dismissal bell jangled. They chanted louder. She'd fake it. One hack. Get it over with. She raised the paddle and swung with the intention of barely striking him. A brittle sound of wood against bone silenced the hawkers. The child was so thin that the paddle landed against his hip bones. Hobo straightened slowly, his eyes welled with tears, but his mouth was molded in a grin. The others crowded around him, back-patting and hand-slapping as if he had just won a marathon. He was still partially bent over, as they herded him out the door with accolades of 'you da man' and 'he's an animal.'

Janice slumped into the teacher's chair. Her throat ached, as she stifled a sob that rose from the center of her chest. She stared at the clay skid marks. Chances are they'd still be there in the morning. She unplugged the fans, draped her jacket across her arm, and switched off the lights. As she locked the door behind her, she heard the sound of running water coming from the far end of the hall.

Returning Student

He was the little shit in class
who mouthed off until I
sent him into the hall,
jacked him against the wall

and inches from his face
told him never to say fuck, shit,
cock sucker or mother fucker
in my classroom. I tapped my finger

like a piledriver against his chest
told him not to show up stoned
ever again. *I'm not stoned* he blurbed.
Planets rotated in his eyes.

He was busted the next month for having sex
in the pool with an under-aged girl.

Damned if he didn't show up
two years later. Marine uniform.
Square-shouldered. Polite as yes sir.
He was off to Afghanistan, asked me

for advice. *You're a vet. What can you
teach me?* Thesis statements and proper
paragraphing hadn't worked.
You're the only one who told me like it is.

I wondered whose voice he was using.
Teach him? I nodded, returned his salute
and said: Keep your ass down.

—*John Davis*

Honest Grading

If I place an F upon his paper
will he seethe in the back of the classroom?

Will he steal into his mother's boudoir,
remove her pearl-handle pistol,
tuck it in his backpack, beside his
graphing calculator?

Will he determine the angle and force
and speed at which a bullet erases a grade?

Will he look me in the eye tomorrow,
slide his hand into his backpack?

Will he shake? Will he break a pencil
as he fingers for the pistol, for the shot
that changes his grade forever?
Will he shoot straight? Will I bleed out
in 97 seconds?

The bell rings. Classes change.
The student walks. He speaks.
Behind him grades collect.
Watch him end this now.

—John Davis

Dropping Out

A. J. Howells

On the roster he was Benjamin Roach, but when I called this name the first day of school, he raised his hand and with a strange level of confidence told me, and thus the rest of the ninth graders, that he went by Ronnie. His classmates snickered and a few rolled their eyes, but I ignored these and scribbled "Ronnie" on the roster, chalking it up to a middle name. Then I noticed his middle initial: D. The new name was a strange request, but Benjamin Roach was an odd name, whereas Ronnie Roach could be the lead singer of a Sex Pistols cover band. Fine by me.

"Kenny?" I called, continuing down the list. Kenny, a scrawny skater kid whose defining quality was abusive sarcasm, raised his hand.

"Actually," he said, "*I* go by Bartholomew." The snickers turned into chuckles. Kenny turned and briefly glared at Ronnie before stretching out his legs and linking his fingers behind his head. Right next to each other on the roster: the resident weirdo and the class clown. My first-year teacher brain stupidly decided to nip the behavior in the bud before getting a better assessment of Kenny, who wasn't so much the class clown as what I'd come to refer to as the "classhole."

"Yeah," I responded, drawing out the word to match his sarcasm, "I'm just going to call you by your last name, 'kay, Solinski?"

Kenny leaped to his feet and shoved aside his desk, which collided with a neighboring peer's, prompting her to release a squeak of fear. "The fuck is that supposed to mean, man?" he demanded, the sarcasm jarringly replaced with pent-up rage. This may have been my first year teaching, but I'd spent the two previous years subbing in inner-city Pittsburgh and four months student teaching on an Indian reservation. Thus, the outburst didn't startle me as much as it forced an internal sigh. *Here we go again.*

"It means you need to get out of my class," I said firmly, but not angrily. Kenny stared at me a few seconds, waiting to see if I'd break eye contact. Then he grabbed his notebook and threw it at me, purposely aiming wide. I've never met a kid intending to hurt a teacher, just ones intending to intimidate, which is hard to accomplish when your notebook opens up and flutters through the air's uncaring resistance. It fell to the ground in a pitiful heap, which brought chuckles back to the classroom. Kenny stomped, toddler-like, out of class, cursing me while I picked up the phone and called the office.

While I was slightly shaken, I was more disappointed that after two years of searching, I'd finally landed a teaching contract, but it was a job where my pupils might still rip into me on a daily basis. After informing the office of the incident, I finished attendance and proceeded to make an even better first impression by monotonously reviewing the syllabus, just like every other teacher in the building. But unlike my colleagues, this review became interesting halfway through my spiel when Mr. McCaig, the assistant principal in charge of ninth grade discipline, popped his head into the room and motioned for me to come to the hallway.

He stood outside with Kenny, who stared at the floor.

"Kenny here," McCaig declared, patting Kenny on the back with a noticeable shove, "is truly sorry he disrupted your class. Would it be okay for him to return?"

It wasn't okay. But it was also my first day teaching, and I'd already kicked a kid out of class, so I couldn't refuse. I nodded and opened the door. McCaig shoved Kenny inside, then motioned for me to walk farther out into the hallway so the kids couldn't hear us.

"Here's the deal," he said, staring down at me from a menacing height, quite the feat considering my six-foot frame. "If it's an emergency, call the office. But don't send a kid out of your room."

This was a bit soon to enter a power struggle. By my fifth and final year at Henderson High, I'd have no problem barking my opinion at the revolving door of administrators, but this was day one. I'd at least try questioning.

"What if a kid is swearing at me and causing a disturbance?"

"Were you in physical danger?"

"He did throw a notebook at me."

McCaig raised an eyebrow, not because of the existence of a projectile, but rather the choice of projectile.

"Did this," he paused here, "*notebook* hurt you?"

"He missed."

"If it's an emergency," he repeated, "call the office. But *don't* send a kid out of your room. I'll come get him." The message was clear. Unless the kid had severed somebody's arms, don't call. And if those arms happened to be mine— well, I wouldn't be able to call, would I? "Understood?" he patronized.

"Yes, sir," I replied. "Have a nice day." I didn't mean it.

"You, too." Neither did he.

I got back to work.

* * *

"Can we talk a minute, man?" Ronnie asked after the rest of the class filed out. My planning block was about to commence, so I had more than a minute. I nodded. "Thanks for what you did earlier," he said.

"The icebreaker activity?" I asked. "You just played on your phone the whole time."

"No," he said. "*That* was dumb. The thing with Kenny. As you can clearly see, he's an asshole." Instinctively, I started to correct Ronnie for his language but then realized I'd stifle whatever he was about to say. "He picks on people who can't defend themselves. Or in my case, he picks on people he doesn't think can defend themselves. If I wanted, I could lay him out. But I don't like hurting people, assholes or otherwise."

This wasn't posturing. Ronnie might have been the emo oddball of the class, but his bulk was primarily muscle. Kenny must have pegged him for a pushover years ago.

"That's good to hear, Ronnie," I said. "I wouldn't want you to get in trouble. And I wouldn't want Kenny to get hurt."

"Not even a little?" he asked, winking.

"Can I ask *you* a question?" I figured not addressing his last question would provide him my answer. Ronnie nodded. "Why do you want to go by Ronnie?"

"There's this old punk band called the Stooges, right?" My jaw dropped a little. "You know them!" Ronnie exclaimed. "Man, I knew you were cool!"

"I didn't think kids listened to the Stooges."

"I'm probably one of the few. So, you know Iggy Pop's real name isn't Iggy Pop? That's not what's on his birth certificate."

"James Osterburg," I said.

"Right!" he exclaimed, excited in a way that indicated he hadn't made a connection with someone in a while, let alone a connection based on something as innocuous as cacophonous music. "But that's such a lame name. James Osterburg couldn't make all this amazing music or do all this crazy shit. But you know who could?"

"Iggy Pop."

"Exactly. So, this little piece of Detroit trailer trash changed his name and ruled the world. Eminem did the same thing. But if Iggy had stayed James Osterburg, or if Eminem stayed Marshall Mathers, where would they be now? So why be Benjamin Roach, when I can be Ronnie Roach? Sounds pretty badass, right? Like someone with a chance."

"A chance at what?"

The torrent of rock history ceased flowing, and Ronnie dropped his eyes. "Well—" he near whispered. He'd assumed I'd know what he'd been referring to, and I did, but I hoped I was wrong. "At life, you know? It's kind of shit wall-to-wall, don't you think?"

It was my turn to consider my words. "It can be. I won't pretend like it can't. But it can be pretty beautiful, too."

"When? And don't give me some lame 'It gets better' bullshit."

I considered this a moment, then gave up. "You mean to tell me a live version of 'T.V. Eye' isn't pretty beautiful?"

Ronnie laughed but didn't agree. Instead, he extended his hand. "It was nice meeting you today," he said. "I'm not really looking forward to coming back to school tomorrow, but I won't mind coming to your class."

"And I won't mind that that's a backhanded compliment."

* * *

Two class sessions later, I reported Ronnie to guidance. Back when I taught English, my students would start the day with ten minutes of journaling. These ten minutes were a sacred time to decompress, or in Kenny's case, write about how much he hated his teachers. (One day he wrote "F U ORDELL" repeatedly for ten minutes. I told him his dedication impressed me.) Ronnie's furious writing, which Kenny would often imitate, was comical. He'd lift his elbow about a foot above his hand, and he'd scribble so quickly I'd expect the page to catch on fire. At the end of each week, I'd ask the students to circle two entries for me to read and comment on. Ronnie's chosen entry was titled "The Cutter's Lullaby," a poem of dubious origin that had gone viral on websites like Wattpad, a writing outlet for depressed teenagers.

I took the notebook to Ronnie's therapeutic support counselor, who took it to his guidance counselor, who started the ball rolling to get Ronnie checked into a hospital by the day's end. Getting parental permission wasn't an issue. His mom told the guidance counselor, "Do whatever you need to do. I thought he'd grown out of that shit."

Ronnie didn't return to school for a week, and when he dragged himself back into my classroom, I told him I was really happy to see him. He ignored me and went to his seat, where he put his head down and left it there, despite my nudges, for nearly a week.

A trait of ninth graders that never ceases to amaze me is the fact that they never seem to grasp the fact that teachers have ears. Nothing whispered in a classroom goes unnoticed by even the most hard-of-hearing among us. This allows us to address serious concerns and let nonsense slide. Perhaps this is why Kenny didn't think I'd hear him whisper, "What's the matter, faggot, your boyfriend leave you?" in Ronnie's ear.

"Out, Kenny," I snapped.

"I don't think so, Ordell," he replied. "*This* is not an emergency situation; therefore, you are not allowed to kick me out of the room."

I smiled at him. All eyes, minus Ronnie's, were on me. "Kenny, you know how you just do whatever you want in here? That's breaking my rules, right?" I pointed to my expectations on the wall, the third of which was "RESPECT: Yourself, Others, The Room."

"Your point?"

"My point is, you're not the only one who can break rules. So, this might not be an emergency situation, but I really don't care. *Get. Out.*" Another staring match ensued, followed by another hasty exit. No projectile this time, though. Just a muttered, "Douchbag."

McCaig arrived outside my classroom about five minutes later, Kenny in tow. "Mr. Ordell, this gentleman is truly sorry—"

"Did he tell you what happened?" I asked. McCaig furrowed his brows. "Kenny," I said, "why don't you run off to the bathroom for a moment?"

Kenny looked at McCaig, who said, "How about you go back to class, Kenny?"

Kenny looked at me and smiled. "I gotta piss anyway," he said. "Thanks, Ordell." This was the only time the kid obeyed one of my requests, and it's only because I was bucking my own superior's orders.

"This isn't an emergency, Mr. Ordell. Explain to me why

you're ignoring the rules."

I explained the situation to McCaig: the poem, mom's lack of concern, the hospital, and Kenny's slur. "If you send him back to this classroom, what's that saying to Benjamin? To the class? To the gay kids?"

Pleasantries were never on the table with McCaig, but after the first incident with Kenny, he refused to make eye contact with me when passing in the hall. But something in his face softened when I told him what Kenny had said. He pinched the skin of his bottom lip between his teeth and pulled on it, then started to speak, but closed his mouth. He turned in the direction of the bathroom and yelled, "Kenny!"

"Yeah?" Kenny called back, his voice echoing off the tile walls.

"When you're done, report back to my office!" Kenny didn't reply. McCaig silently walked away, and I returned to my classroom and got back to work.

I never needed to kick Kenny out of class again. He wasn't pleasant, but he was no longer nearly as overt in his misbehavior. For the rest of the year, I attributed this to McCaig, but I wasn't sure why. My interactions with McCaig remained the same. If he saw me in the distance, he'd duck into someone's classroom until I passed.

At the end of the school year, the English teachers sat around a campfire at our department head's house, passing the theater teacher's phone around the circle. It got to me last, so I had seen all of my colleagues' reactions before seeing the cause. The men generally covered their eyes with the back of a hand. Some of the women would do the same, but some of their eyes bulged, followed by an approving nod. Then the phone was in my hand, and I was looking at a well-endowed college student performing acrobatic tasks on a gay porno site. The student's last name was the unoriginal moniker "Johnson," and we'd all previously seen his framed photograph in a certain assistant principal's office window. We knew his real last name was McCaig.

Ronnie kept his head up after this incident, but it was another week or two before he would engage in conversation. The bell rang one day, and he remained at his desk while the other students filed out.

"You didn't have to report me, you know," he said, voice cracking. He clearly hadn't spoken *at all* over the past couple weeks.

I sat next to him and said, "I did, though. I'm a mandated reporter."

Ronnie waived off the explanation. "That's a very *adult* thing to say." He nearly spat the word "adult," as if it were a pejorative.

"Look, Ronnie. If I hadn't reported this, and you went home and killed yourself, what then? I'm supposed to live the rest of my life knowing I could have stopped it?"

He looked me in the eyes for the first time. "You couldn't stop it, though. Not if I were determined to do it, *which I wasn't*. I didn't even write that poem."

"I'm not sorry for what I did," I said, standing. "And I'm not sorry that you're back. I am, however, sorry to see those scabs on your knuckles."

"You noticed?" he asked, the shadow of a smirk appearing on his face.

"I also noticed how quiet it was in class today without Kenny here." This was a rare absence. There's an unwritten rule in teaching that the kids who cause the most trouble will be in your class every day, and the ones that need to be there the most rarely show. "How is he?"

"You gonna report me for this, too?"

"Guess that depends on what you did to him."

"Kenny's fine. We ride the same bus, though we get off at different stops. Yesterday he got off at my stop and started following me home, talking more of that homophobic shit— the kid is unbelievably repressed, you know? I almost feel bad for him, but not bad enough to keep putting up with it. Pacifists have their limits. Anyway, there's a shallow grave behind the Seven-Eleven."

"Ronnie—"

"Cool it, Ordell. You know I'm kidding. He's nursing a black eye and a split lip. Probably wanted to heal up a bit before showing his face around here. I suspect he won't give either of us any more issues."

"I wouldn't hold your breath, Ronnie. And please don't do it again. You did exactly what he wanted you to."

The tardy bell for the next class sounded, and Ronnie stood. "It took me this long to take a stand. I'll go back to spinelessness for a while.

"Anyway, *you* standing up for me meant more than anything I could have done for myself. There are teachers out there that pretend they don't hear that shit. They just keep on with their lesson. So, despite you sending me to the psych ward, you're still cool." The smirk turned into a grin. "I guess."

"Get out of here, Ronnie," I said, laughing.

"Can I get a pass?"

* * *

One of the consistent trends in education is that the average teacher lasts three to five years before changing careers. Many of those who remain wear the title of teacher as if it were a purple heart, and they'll let you know every chance they get just how soul-crushing their job truly is, but that it's worth it just to make a difference in their students' lives.

You do *not* want to get stuck at a dinner party with these people.

I'll grant them something, though. Watching students evolve as rapidly as they do across the high school grades does make up for a lot of the field's bullshit. There's a huge jump in maturity from ninth to tenth grade, and by eleventh they either dig their heels in and conclude that, since the cards are stacked so highly against them, failure is the only way to survive, or they decide to set fire to these barriers.

Kenny was in the former group. The day he turned eighteen, he filed the necessary papers to drop out. Months later, he ended up in the local section of the newspaper after raping a minor in a neighboring state. The shelter of a high school could only protect the world from him for so long.

Ronnie, in typical fashion, didn't belong to either group, and he cycled through different personalities at record speed. He quit the emo gig after a particularly embarrassing incident. During one of my Shakespeare lectures, a student timidly raised her hand. When she got my attention, she pointed at Ronnie, who had silently spit up a small stream of vomit, which had pooled into a tiny puddle on his desk. The rest of the class quickly realized what had happened, and bedlam erupted as they tried to get away from him. I grabbed a garbage can and handed it to Ronnie, but he batted it away and stood to run to the bathroom. The moment he stepped toward the door, a geyser erupted, and he futilely covered his mouth to stop the vomit, which spilled through his fingers. He made it to the hallway and ran for the bathroom. The sound of heaves and splashes echoed off the brick walls of the hallway.

I called the nurse for Ronnie then the office for the puke. "Better send a custodian," I told the latter. "Maybe five of them." Being a rookie teacher, I was convinced my lecture was far more important than it actually was, so instead of trying to locate an empty room, I pushed the desks to the furthest wall from the vomit and continued lecturing while a custodian cleaned the puke.

I went to the nurse's office after class. Ronnie was still there, as was his day therapist, Trista.

"How's he holding up?" I asked her.

Trista sat in the nurse's waiting area and sighed. "He's not. It's been a while since the suicide watch, and I really hope this doesn't change that. Especially since he's alone."

"He's alone?"

"When Ronnie leaves here, he goes home to a mother he despises, and, unfortunately, the feeling is mutual. They stopped speaking to each other months ago, but he doesn't have any friends, so he's stuck there. Whatever he says to me as he leaves here are his last words until he gets back the next day."

"If he even bothers coming to school," I added. Trista nodded.

"Then there's the weekends. Occasionally, he'll leave his house and walk around town, but most of the time he stays in his room. His mom stays in hers."

"Jesus. What's her deal?"

"She's got a slew of undiagnosed 'deals.' About a week ago, she left. And since they're not talking to each other, Ronnie has no idea where she went. He just woke up one morning, and she was gone."

"Sounds like a lucky break."

"For a day or two, but he's a nervous wreck now, as evidenced by today. Ronnie might hate his mom *and* his life, but uncertainty is unbearable. It's ripping him apart."

"Can I talk to him?" I asked. I didn't know what I would say, and it wouldn't have helped. Trista shook her head.

"He's just wallowing back there," she said. "Won't let anyone check on him. This one is going to stick with him for a long time."

But it didn't. Ronnie missed the next week's worth of classes, but when he finally returned, he'd ditched the guyliner and dyed his hair blond. He'd replaced the leather jacket with a denim one, under which was a tie-dyed tee, homemade. Our meaningful conversations abruptly ended, replaced by the vacuity of a stoner's personality. His final research essay was evidence of this, as it was a garbled mess with a picture of the chemical breakdown of marijuana in the header where his name should have been ("It better conveys my personality than my name") and an incoherent argument for the legalization of marijuana ("DUIs will decrease cuz there wont be a reeson to driving anymore"), complete with the obligatory "it cures cancer" argument of teenage stoners nationwide. Nearly every day, I tried to speak meaningfully with him, but his armor was now impenetrable. "I'm cool now, man," he'd say. "Not a care in the world."

* * *

Ronnie passed freshmen English, but he did not pass sophomore English. Not after his first attempt, or his second attempt, or his third attempt. He started a fourth attempt with the only remaining tenth grade teacher but disappeared shortly thereafter. I assumed he'd dropped out until I saw him in my neighborhood, walking home from the bus stop.

Ronnie had been a city kid his whole life, and while "the city" consisted of thirty-thousand residents, the surrounding county was quite sparse, and my county neighborhood, which consisted of ten miles of dirt roads switchbacking up the side of a mountain, was the most sparsely populated part of the area. It was a neighborhood for three types of people: 1) marijuana harvesters, 2) misanthropes, 3) teachers. The teachers were drawn to the affordable, but somehow not-meth-lab-chic, housing. I existed solely in the third category. Ronnie was in the first two.

I saw Ronnie three times before he disappeared completely. The first was when I noticed him walking away from the bus stop. I was driving home, so I pulled up next to him and rolled the window down. He'd been walking with a determined look on his face, his headphone volume cranked up to the maximum level. When he turned and saw me, his grave countenance broke into a grin.

"Hey, man!" he exclaimed. "You live around here?"

"I do. Are you still in school?"

"Yeah, man! County now. They got me to twelfth grade, so all I gotta do is finish out the year."

"That's good to hear, Ronnie. I'm proud of you."

"Merry Christmas, okay?" he said. I nodded and wished him one as well, then drove away. Two things were clear.

One, he didn't remember my name. And two, he did remember me as one of the teachers preventing him from getting to twelfth grade. Maybe it's because I'd been in a car, so the awkward nature of having a conversation in the middle of the road limited our discussion, but deep down, I knew our relationship—always strained by me adhering to the moral imperatives of my job—had been irreparably damaged. He was like the family member nice enough to send you a Christmas card, but wise enough never to engage in a conversation outside this formality.

The second to last time I ran into Ronnie was while I was training for a half-marathon. I rounded a corner of one of the mountain roads and spotted a little black dot in the distance. I couldn't visually determine this was Ronnie, but I could aurally determine, as he was bellowing, "I don't know, but I've been told! The Marine Corps is mighty bold!" The closer I ran, the better I could make out his stiff marching. Once I got close enough, he stopped shouting, pulled out his headphones, and called me over.

"Hey, man!" he called. "I'm training!"

I stopped to catch my breath. "Me, too," I replied, "but it looks like you're training for the service."

"Hell yeah, I am. Just gotta pass the tests and I'm out of here. I finally graduated!"

I clasped him on the shoulder. "Always knew you had it in you, Ronnie."

"And now I've got *this* in me. Anything I want to do, I can do, you know?"

I couldn't agree with him. Ronnie had spent the better part of high school killing as many brain cells as possible. I wanted his success, but I just couldn't see him passing any of the tests. Instead of faux encouragement, I decided to instead throw him another life preserver for when this venture failed. "Good luck to you. Ronnie, where do you live?"

"Over on Opossum with mom's ex-boyfriend. The only one of them ever worth a damn." I lived on Opossum, though I'd never seen him walking it.

"I'm the first house on the left as soon as you turn onto Opossum," I told him. "If you ever need anything, come see me."

"Thanks, man," he said. He paused a second, perhaps to try and recall my name. "Gotta get back to training. SOUND OFF, ONE, TWO!" I didn't think I'd ever see him again.

And I might not have. That very well could have been the last time I saw Ronnie. It certainly was the last time I spoke with him.

Around dusk on Christmas Day, as my extended family sat around the living room watching my two-year-old son sit among wrapping paper wreckage and play with his new toys, we started hearing someone belting out a Clash song outside, perhaps a destitute drunk. There seemed to be plenty of them in the neighborhood.

"I'M SO BORED WITH THE U! S! A! I'M SO BORED WITH THE U! S! A!"

I opened the front door a crack but couldn't see anyone. The voice, however, was getting closer. "Merry Christmas to all!" it screamed. "Unless you're fucking *poor!*" Ronnie, who should have been my first guess, didn't come to mind—the voice didn't match. Granted, it was a drunk and wavering voice, but the anger held a tinge of threat. Ronnie wouldn't hurt a fly, unless that fly's name was Kenny.

When the drunk finally appeared at the crest of the road, Ronnie still didn't pop into my mind. It was close enough to dark that I still couldn't make out the face. I could, however, make out the bottle he clutched. He would stop walking between curses, take a swig, then go back to stumbling and screaming. "You gotta die for the government—that's SHIT!" Anti-Flag. Another punk anthem. One quite obscure compared to the stylings of Joe Strummer. Now Ronnie came to mind.

The man passed our house and headed up a neighbor's wooded lane. He pounded the front door with the bottom of his bottle. "Merry Christmas to all, except me!"

I closed the door and turned to my wife. "I think that's Ronnie. He's going to get shot." In our neighborhood, I was fairly confident we were the only residents without an NRA membership. We didn't own guns but figured we were secure knowing everyone else did. If the neighbor was home, and he appeared to be, he might fire a shotgun blast through his front door. "Should I go talk to him?"

My wife didn't say anything. Instead, she turned and looked at our boy, who looked at me and asked, "What wrong?"

I keep telling myself that the drunk might not have been Ronnie, but I know it was. I keep telling myself he didn't think he was pounding on *my* front door, but I know he did. I keep telling myself I could have told him something that would have helped him, but I know I couldn't have.

Instead, I called the cops, who told me I was the latest in a string of phone calls from my neighborhood reporting the same incident. After a while, the screaming stopped, though I never heard a cop car. I keep telling myself if the cops *did* pick up Ronnie, they pitied him and took him straight home, but I know this isn't the case. I keep telling myself I'll see him again, but a year has passed, and I haven't. I've pushed through the three-to-five year barrier, and I keep telling myself I'll make it to ten years of teaching, but I know I won't.

Charm Disarmed

No argument, no fight,
last night the School Board
funded new staff development
out of a thin budget:
teachers trained to shoot—
more school safety,
more guns on campus.

My student Rob, spine
in shards—staff
griped about his
smelly colostomy bag—
educated with an
armor-piercing bullet.

Rosa dropped in the
parking lot,
an abandoned doll,
freshman boy braggadocio
with his father's gun.

Forty-two years fostering
children, trust, and learning,
I cannot watch the burning
of a child, nor light the match.

—*Victoria Crawford*

Lost In Translation

Miriam Thor

"If a crocodile and a hippo got in a fight, which one do you think would win?"

Mindy Patterson voiced that question, then did her best not to blush as twenty eighth graders stopped trying to solve world problems and turned to stare at her. As a sign language interpreter, it was her duty to interpret everything her student signed into spoken English, regardless of how...random it was. After three years working in the school system, Mindy was used to the rest of the class mistaking her student's comments for her own. That didn't mean it wasn't still a bit awkward, though.

"Tyler," Mrs. Hodges said sternly. "We're working on solving word problems using equations, *not* African zoology. You need to pay attention."

Mindy interpreted the rebuke, making sure to simplify the language. If she left words like equations and zoology in it, there was no chance Tyler would understand its meaning. When she finished, Tyler smirked but begrudgingly went back to work.

Mindy sighed. If he was behaving this way in first period, it didn't bode well for the rest of his day. And since her job was to accompany Tyler to all of his classes and facilitate communication, it didn't bode well for her day either.

As she mentally prepared herself for what lay ahead, Tyler waved his hand to get her attention. When she looked at him, he signed, *What does p-u-d-d-l-e mean?*

Mindy studied him for a moment, trying to decide if he actually needed to know the word 'puddle' to solve a word problem or if he was just messing around. Since his brown eyes lacked any hint of mischief, she concluded it was the former and briefly defined it for him. When she finished, Tyler looked back at his worksheet with a nod, and Mindy pulled out the small notebook she carried in her purse. She added 'puddle' to the list of vocabulary words she worked on with Tyler every day after lunch.

Skimming over the list, Mindy shook her head. Eighth graders should already know words like buckle and rust, but due to his hearing loss and many other factors, Tyler's language was at about a second-grade level. And though she was trying her best to help him close that gap, some days, like today, she wondered if it was even possible.

Maybe I should go back to working on vocabulary between classes, she thought. Tyler would hate it, but it might be worth it in the long run.

The bell rang, interrupting Mindy's thoughts.

"Hand me your worksheet on your way out the door," Mrs. Hodges said. Mindy shoved her notebook back into her purse and quickly interpreted the instructions. Though she knew Tyler could see her hands moving out of the corner of his eye, he didn't look up. Instead, he put his worksheet in his folder and unzipped his backpack. Aggravated, Mindy tapped his desk.

Mrs. Hodges said to give the worksheet to her on your way out, she signed.

Tyler glanced toward the door and saw the other students handing their papers to the teacher, then pulled his out of his folder and crammed the rest of his stuff in his bag. As he walked over and turned in his work, Mindy wondered if she'd done the right thing. Technically, interpreters were supposed to sign exactly what the teacher said. No more, no less. Tyler knew he was supposed to look at her when she started interpreting, and if he chose not to, that was his fault, and he needed to face the consequences for that, just like hearing students did when they chose to ignore the teacher.

As she dodged teenagers on her way to the gym, Mindy frowned. All that was good in theory. The problem was that Tyler didn't care about his grades or taking responsibility for his actions. He'd been punished many times in the past and hadn't seemed to learn anything. Mindy figured that by giving him a nudge here and there, Tyler would at least get credit for the work he actually took the time to do. That might help him pass the eighth grade, but was it encouraging him to continue being irresponsible? Mindy wrestled with that question every day.

When she reached the gym, Mindy saw squishy balls lined up around the basketball court and groaned. Dodgeball? Really? This just wasn't her day.

As the last few students trickled into the gym, Mindy leaned against a wall, close enough to Tyler that he could see her if she started interpreting but far enough that she couldn't hear the conversation he was having with his friend. Tyler needed an interpreter for large, group settings, especially when the speaker was moving around, but one-on-one, it wasn't usually necessary. Tyler wasn't completely deaf, so between what he heard and what he lipread, he could understand most of what someone said. Mindy knew he would understand even more if he wore his hearing aids, but she had given up on winning that battle a long time ago. As for speaking, Tyler was usually intelligible, although it wasn't uncommon for people to ask Mindy to interpret his "English" into better English.

After the bell rang, Coach Baldwin called the roll, then explained the rules for free-for-all dodgeball, a game he'd invented where half the students stood along the edges of the basketball court and threw balls at the remaining students in the middle. Mindy interpreted the rules in detail, despite the fact that Tyler knew them and wasn't paying any attention to her. Then, Coach Baldwin divided the class into two groups. Tyler was sorted into the group that had to stand around the court, so Mindy followed him to the spot he chose and positioned herself several yards in front of him while he picked up a ball. Coach Baldwin always gave some last-minute instructions right before he blew the whistle to begin the game, and Mindy had to make sure Tyler knew what they were.

When all the students were in place, Coach Baldwin yelled, "Remember not to aim for anyone's head!" and blew the whistle. Mindy interpreted his words as fast as she could, then ran off the court, dodging the balls that Tyler and those near him had thrown. She felt one ball hit her ankle from behind just as she made it out of bounds.

"Sorry, Mrs. Patterson!" a boy yelled from the other side of the gym.

"It's okay," she yelled back, moving farther out of harm's way. She spent the rest of the period sitting in the relative safety of the bleachers, keeping an eye out for stray balls and only getting up twice when the coach gave instructions. A lot of people would've been bored sitting by themselves and watching middle schoolers play dodgeball, but Mindy didn't mind. It was the closest thing she got to a break.

When the bell rang, Mindy reluctantly headed to English, her least favorite class of the day. For reasons she didn't understand, Tyler didn't like his English teacher, Ms. Lewis, so he did everything he could to disrupt her class. It made for a very long period for everyone.

Mindy entered the classroom and sat in her usual chair. Then, she picked a spot on the back wall to stare at while she interpreted. The moment Ms. Lewis started teaching, Mindy fixed her eyes on that spot and didn't look away from it for the next hour while Tyler folded paper airplanes, made inappropriate comments, and tried to see how hard he had to blow to knock over his binder. Ms. Lewis reprimanded him a few times, and Mindy dutifully interpreted her words. But they both knew it was pointless. Tyler had been behaving this way for the last four months and was highly unlikely to stop any time soon.

Mindy couldn't help but be relieved when the bell rang, signaling the end of third period. She grabbed her purse and headed to science, glad to have the worst of her day behind her.

"Good morning," Leah said as Mindy walked into the science classroom and sat down. Mindy smiled. Most of Tyler's teachers were simply her co-workers, but Leah Dixon had become a friend.

"Good morning," Mindy replied, hanging her purse on the back of her chair. Leah eyed her speculatively.

"Rough day?" she asked.

Mindy shrugged. "I've had worse."

Leah rolled her eyes. "With that reasoning, even terrible days can't be called bad."

Mindy nodded thoughtfully. Her friend had a point.

"Good morning, Tyler," Leah said, turning to look at him with a glowing smile.

"Good morning, Ms. Dixon. Guess what I did last night?" Tyler asked and launched into a story about finding a huge lizard in his backyard and trying to feed it a cricket.

Leah nodded when he finished. "Sounds like a lot of fun," she said. "If you see that lizard again, you'll have to take a picture of it and show me." Then, she walked to the front of the room and began the day's lesson.

For the next half hour, Tyler was attentive and respectful. He watched Mindy as she interpreted the lesson about layers of the earth and even asked a couple of relevant questions.

When Leah instructed the class to do a worksheet independently, Mindy set her hands in her lap and watched Tyler work quietly at his desk. It never ceased to amaze her how he could flip an internal switch and transform into the ideal student when he wanted to. Tyler had a connection with Leah Dixon, and his desire for her to like him inspired him to do his best. Mindy wished he would try even half this hard when she worked on vocabulary with him, but she knew better than to expect it. Mindy wasn't sure exactly what quality Leah possessed that made Tyler like her, but she knew she didn't have it. Tyler was sure to be as obstinate today as he always was.

Mindy heaved a sigh. She had tried everything she could think of to help Tyler learn, and she hoped and prayed that he'd be able to get a job he enjoyed in the future. But for that to happen, his language had to improve. Mindy had tried to convince Tyler of that in every way imaginable, but so far, it didn't seem to have done any good. It was like they spoke different languages. Mindy hadn't given up; she never would. But her hope dwindled a little more every day.

"Okay everyone, pass your papers to one person at your

table," Leah said, snapping Mindy back to the present. "It's almost time to go."

Mindy interpreted the instructions mechanically. After Tyler handed his paper to the boy sitting next to him, he raised his hand.

"Yes, Tyler?" Leah said, walking over to stand near him.

"Why this has rust on it?" he asked, pointing to the metal part of his chair.

"Because it's old," Leah said simply, taking the papers from the boy next to him. Mindy interpreted the reply, doing her best to hide her shock. Tyler remembered the word 'rust' well enough to use it independently? That meant she could check it off her list. With a smile, Mindy took out her notebook and did just that. Then, she skimmed over the list like she had that morning, this time noting the ones she'd checked off, instead of the ones she hadn't. Tyler really had made progress this year, even if it wasn't as much as she would've liked.

"You can line up for lunch," Leah told her class. As the students eagerly obeyed, Mindy walked over and grabbed her and Leah's lunches from the refrigerator in the back of the classroom. Then, she joined her friend next to the door.

"Now, *walk* to the cafeteria," Leah said. When the last student had filed out the door, she took her lunch from Mindy and said, "Thanks."

"No problem," Mindy replied, and the two of them started walking toward the cafeteria together. When they reached the door to the teacher's lounge, Mindy paused. "I'll join you in a minute," she said.

Leah chuckled. "I figured it was a Pepsi day," she said, continuing down the hallway. "See you soon."

Mindy nodded and went into the lounge. She dug some change out of her purse and used it to buy a Pepsi from the vending machine. With the can in hand, she headed toward the cafeteria, shaking her head. The eighth-grade teachers had all noticed that she only drank soda when she needed a pick-me-up, so they could tell what kind of day she was having just by what beverage she drank at lunch. Mindy hadn't decided if she should find it amusing or sad that she was that predictable.

When she entered the cafeteria, Mindy glanced at where Tyler usually sat and found him making a rope out of plastic fork wrappers. She sighed deeply, grateful for the caffeine she was about to ingest, and walked toward the teacher table, mentally preparing herself for the second half of her day.

Innocence Lost

Early morning of that 87-hour day,
planes crashed into impossibly tall
buildings in downtown Manhattan.
From the hill, a cloud of black smoke
confirmed the horror broadcast
over and over and over.

Nearby elementary school teachers
could only imagine the fate of
loved ones working on Wall Street.
Emerging from restrooms with
red-rimmed eyes and runny noses,
they plastered smiles on adult faces to
meet eager young faces of students,
who would not be told of the terror.

Parents came to take their children home,
compelled to reunite family
for hugs and tears together.
Remaining children were left to assume
there were an unusual number
of dentist appointments that day.

News reports compounded fear.
People had jumped from burning towers
to escape intense heat.
Emergency responders were overcome
with smoke and dust.
The towers had collapsed.
Hundreds were missing.
There were no survivors.

In fifth grade, Mary wrote a poem about her dog.
Tony finally understood regrouping and
was able to show his solution on the board.
Ellie read *Hop on Pop* to her Kindergarten.
No one got in a fight on the playground.
Three girls and two boys visited the nurse.
The music teacher cried during third period chorus.

The school day ended with students lined up
to board buses, or get in their parents' cars,
to take them home—
to news no one wanted them to hear,
to pictures no one wanted them to see,
to a reality no one wanted to acknowledge.

A parent asked, "What do I say to my children?"
The only answer that came, "Tell them
there is evil in the world,
and you are here to protect them."
It seemed an insufficient answer
to an unanswerable question
on a day of unspeakable tragedy.

—*Sheryl Guterl*

Abdicated

Linda Sánchez

My first impression of Phillip was that he was blessed with ignorance. He seemed perfectly equipped for survival, a great wall of naiveté shielding him from his environment. I couldn't tell if his ignorance came from his youth entirely or if it was inbred in him, like his slightly receding hairline or his annoyingly lanky limbs. He was twenty-something, the age I hate most.

Roberta introduced me to Phillip after an excruciatingly long and intense interview in her tiny, windowless office. My armpits and forehead moist from fielding questions, I followed her down a concrete-walled hallway full of rowdy youths loosely grouped in twos and threes—many of whom she greeted affectionately—and through several locked doors that Roberta opened from a set of keys on a lanyard around her neck. Finally, we arrived at the Alternative Education classroom to meet Phillip, the other teacher—my potential colleague.

The day hadn't begun well at all. The drive into the city had been brutal. Ten years in the suburbs had wiped out my memories of this kind of morning commute. But I braved the potholes; the aggressive, terse driving; the sudden unexplained traffic backups; and the darting pedestrians and finally parked in an overpriced lot all the while feeling like my Grammie during her weekly outing to Stop & Shop: confused, unsteady, and with a deep, instinctual longing for home.

Then the meeting with Roberta had been so awkward. We both knew I was overqualified for the job, most likely overqualified for her job as well. Her questions, posed with a lilting Spanish accent and an achingly open expression in her eyes, all ultimately asked the same thing: "Why?" After the first few responses, I could hear the stiffness in my voice. It was growing hot in the airless office; I felt too big for the chair. I wondered if I could explain to this stranger how the small ad in the Help Wanted section had captivated me, sending me back again and again to the Sunday paper, an uncomfortable excitement building in me. I knew the pay would be minuscule, the hours long, and the benefits nonexistent, but the idea of returning to this world of impassioned hopeful work sent a pinball of possibility careening through my past, knocking enough bumpers that I found myself writing a cover letter and considering which of my drab, tired outfits could pass as a resume suit. Getting the call from Roberta and then preparing for the interview caused something else to stir in me, something I hadn't felt for years.

Led by this feeling and totally unprepared to come face to face with my past, I met Phillip. We were all contrasts: I, thick and pasty in a gray knit suit, maroon cardigan, and heavy black shoes; he, in low-slung jeans and a white button-down. I was accessorized by a stunning silver and jet necklace, a gift from a grateful student at last year's commencement. Phillip's only accessory was an utter conviction in his ability to change the world. He knew nothing, and I knew too much. In another setting, we might have a lot to teach each other, but I felt ridiculous being interviewed by this very young and inexperienced man. I was a caricature of an interviewee, thick and clumsy, a stiff smile frozen on my face, not knowing what to do with my hands. Phillip explained the day-to-day of the position, the role of informal teacher and guide as students—often mandated by courts and parole officers—worked toward GEDs, English language skills, basic life skills, and anger management. Meanwhile, a few students, jeans with crotches hung by their knees and sideways baseball caps, strutted around the room grooving to iPods. Others sat hunched at round tables, chewing on pencils and examining the work in front of them. They were the polar opposite of the well-dressed, clean-cut students I saw every day on the lush green campus of the prep school that I have called academic home for the last ten years. One of the students, Dylan, a dark-skinned Latino, kept up a steady stream of loud banter, interrupted us at every turn, openly mocked Phillip, and ignored me completely, dismissing me as irrelevant. I didn't understand all of what he said, but I found him crass and rude, and I had to hold my tongue and my facial muscles back from telling him what I thought of him. As I nervously fingered my necklace, I looked inside and felt a cavernous lack of compassion that shocked and chilled me.

I could tell that Phillip was uncomfortable, but he was proud, too. He had claimed ownership over this rowdy group of youths, and in that ownership, he also held great hope for them. I watched him closely as he waited patiently for Dylan to stop his rap. I could see the beginnings of frustration and the traces of exhaustion in his eyes. Phillip, by his own admission, was new to the workforce and had only been in this position for four months. Was it my imagination, or was the slightest trace of cynicism already threatening to curl his lip?

I was suddenly exhausted from the day. I knew I couldn't open myself back up to that hope, that possibility that I could make a difference. I had gone too far, had allowed cynicism to build too much of a stronghold where hope once nested. The optimistic graduate, the enthusiastic Peace Corps volunteer, the impassioned youth worker I had once been were gone. I remembered why I had changed my path so long ago, all the while feeling like a sell-out; I had set my goals too high. I had realized that I couldn't change the world, that there was nothing I could do to help the Dylan's of the world. I could only help myself. So, I did.

An hour with Roberta in her office, another with Phillip in the classroom, and I finally escaped. Any scrap of ambiguity about my interest in this job disappeared as I exited the building onto the filthy street and felt the first panic about the safety of my car that I had had in years. I wanted my suburban home; my respectful, submissive students; and the terra firma of mediocrity. As I drove home, tired and drained, I fingered the glistening necklace at my throat. I tugged at it, but it didn't give. I knew I would never repeat that commute again.

A Triptych from the Teacher

Thursday, 3:28 p.m.

Don't be fooled, kid.
  I count down the clock
  as much as you.

Especially when it's
Thursday, 5th period and
31 fifteen-year-olds and I sit
in a room overripe with either
teen hormones or the garbage
I forgot to take out.

Thursdays are the worst.
Minds mushy from four days
of braining, the weekend
so close
we can nearly taste it and yet
we know we have to come back
in the morning.
One more day, one more try.

"Ah, Mrs. P!" you cry,
"I've got three more years. I'm
so done!
I just want to get on with my
real life, ya know?"
Yeah, kid. I know. Believe me.
But somehow my real life
means returning to high school
year after year after year.

Sixteen more to go for me.

Tick, tick, tock.
3:29

Forgive my snark.
It's Thursday.

Monday, 8:52 a.m.

Don't be fooled, kid.
     My eyes are just as bleary as yours
     under my Monday Morning perk.

Especially when I crammed in a
week's worth of living into a
two-day weekend, and while
I no longer lug 200 papers
back and forth from home, the
digital weight of the workload
weighs no less on my mind.

Mondays are all right.
Mind fresh and body rested,
I face 5 days of lessons,
25 class periods, 216 students,
1 case of plagiarism,
and 5 kids wondering how they can
get their grades up when they haven't
turned in any work.
One day in, four more to go.

"Ah, Mrs. P!" you cry,
"I don't really wake up till
2nd period. Do I really have to
read this poem? I mean, it's a poem!"
Yeah, kid. You do. But maybe,
just maybe,
this poem will really wake you up,
make you feel, make you think,
make you question.
You flip open your laptop
and begin to read.

Tick, tick, tock.
8:53

Forgive my zeal.
It's Monday.

Tuesday, 11:41 a.m.

Don't be fooled, kid.
    I might seem like a blasé adult,
    but I live for this.

Especially when we sit
side by side over a notebook
you finally wrote in when you
thought your friends weren't looking,
in a room humming with
pencil tapping and keyboard clacking.

These days are the best.
Mind unleashed by a lucky prompt
that somehow unlocked the voice
you kept hidden through
7 months of time together until
today, this morning,
when the bell rang and, inexplicably,
you were brave enough to try.

"Ah, Mrs. P!" you cry,
"I don't know how to do this.
I've done themes and thesis statements,
but I've never written anything that
sounds like me, ya know?"
Yeah, kid. I do. Even now.
Finding your voice is a lifelong pursuit,
a journey I'm still taking myself.
But I can guide you.

Tick, tick, tock.
I don't care about the time.

Forgive my disregard.
I've got work to do.

—*Julie Pullman*

There Are No

Stupid Questions

Matthew E. Henry

Second-semester seniors are always looking for shortcuts. With essays this means the creative borrowing of antecedent information, without appropriate citation or attribution: they plagiarize and hope they don't get caught. Often it's only a couple of sentences shining like a diamond of advanced diction and imagery in the rough of a C- page. Sometimes it's a whole page or two. But when it came time to cheat, Kerri embraced her year's ethos: "go big or go home!" and I find her entire *Hamlet* term paper online.

Without naming names, I caution the entire class about these problems: meet with me in private, own your action, and we can talk about how to salvage your final grade. Or don't and take your chances. Some students maintain eye contact. Others become preoccupied with their shoes, the lint on their sleeves. Kerri stares out the window until the bell rings. Fifteen minutes later one of her friends re-enters the room, not to confess, but to inform me that Kerri is in the guidance office crying, saying she won't graduate because the evil black man has accused her of cheating! I sigh.

As my informant leaves the room, Kerri enters asking to see her paper. I sift through the stack, pretending hers is not on top, casually asking if something is wrong. She looks upset. "I just want to know my grade." I hand her a stapled set of papers with no marks on the page. "Is this yours?" With a glance she confirms that it is. I shift my weight and the stack of papers falls from my desk to the ground. I bend to collect them, rising with one in hand. "I'm sorry Kerri. Are you sure that's yours? This paper has your name at the top." Her eyes widen and dart from her hand to mine. "The paper you're holding is one I found on the internet." I retrieve it from her hands and hold it beside the other. We play a quick *Highlights* game of "spot the differences." One of us loses. "Kerri, can you please explain this?" She runs out of the room.

"She did *not* plagiarize!" It has been over a month since her daughter was caught cheating, but the asininity of Kerri's mother will not abate. At our many meetings she has become quite adept at answering for her silent daughter. She can never explain why the two papers are identical in every way, but she is confident that the fault is mine, and hints that another teacher, a less "urban" individual, would understand. My acceptably white department head is seated at the head of the table and is visibly uncomfortable. He attempts to defuse the situation when she adds, "And she should be rewarded!" without a hint of irony. As a first year teacher, I instinctively know it is not acceptable to violently flip the table while screaming, *Rewarded for what?! Cheating?!* That would be unprofessional and inappropriate. I take a deep breath, count to five, regain some measure of composure, and ask, "Rewarded for what? Cheating?" As the incoherent barrage of her response washes over me, I begin to understand Kerri's actions more clearly, seeing her past and future reflected in her mother's face and facsimile of sense. The apple hasn't fallen near the tree, it's levitating.

My department head silently surveys the scene. He's quitting at the end of the year—a few weeks from now—and returning to the parentless simplicity of university teaching. In private, he's told me the outcome is ultimately my call, but he wants the whole thing to just go away. I never asked what he meant by "thing." We both would like Kerri to admit her wrong, but only I find this a hill worth dying on. I can only be lied to for so long. This will be the last meeting. Kerri will answer for herself.

"Did you plagiarize?" It's become my mantra.
    "I didn't plagiarize."
    "Why are these two papers the same?"
    "I didn't plagiarize."
    "Then *why* are these two papers the same?"
    "I didn't plagiarize."
    "Then why are these two papers *exactly* the same?"
    "I didn't plagiarize."
    Time for a new tact: dumb it down and turn it up.
    "Did you find this paper in a book and type it up?"
    "No."
    "Did you find this paper on a website and print it out?"
    "No."
    "Did you find this paper on a website, then copy and paste it into your document?"
    "No."
    "Did you pay someone else to type it for you, after finding it on a website or in a book?"
    "No."
    "Did an alien from outer space, possibly a monkey, inhabit your brain and force you to do only God knows what, including, but not limited to, plagiarizing this paper, but you have no memory of the horrible events that befell you that night, due to whatever physical or chemical blocks it inserted into your head?"
    "Uhm . . . no?"

I sit back in my chair and gesture to the two papers all four of us admit are almost identical.

"You have got to give me something to work with here."

And she did.

Idiocy amazes me in bright carnival colors: the swirling greens, red, and blues of mentalities mismatched like kindergarten socks, the pre-school propensity to mix orange juice and milk. Even a fool is counted wise when she holds her peace, and a chicken's heart will eventually accept his head's knowledge and fall silent. But there are moments that define a person's ability to be surprised. Thankfully, mine arrived so early in my career.

"I found it online, read through it, copied and pasted it into Microsoft Word, printed it out on paper, re-read it, retyped it back into my computer, printed it out again, and then passed it in."

"..."

"I didn't plagiarize."

The silence is broken by my department head's sigh, before Kerri's mother smiles, nods, and asks,

"So, you'll let her pass, right?"

To My Student Being Deported

My training conditions me to not judge
Your total lack of observable interest
In my class or anything I say—sometimes
Miracles emerge with love and patience.
Each time I ask when you will turn in
Your missing work so you can pass,
You politely lie that it will all be in
At the start of next week, and of course
I am wise to never hold my breath
For every next week that passes.
Your name pegged you to the hard
Side of the Adriatic, flesh trafficking
In the streets of Tirana transformed
Into a Coney Island restaurant on Gratiot
Or a party storefront off Chalmers.
I said I stay away from judgment,
But after class one day you approach
Me in the hall pleading a favor.
Not the extension on late work I'd hoped
For or a chance to negotiate a D-, nothing
So meaningless as that. No, it seems
That Uncle Sam has caught up with
All your changed addresses, the weeks
In an uncle's basement, two months
In the storage room above the used
Car dealership, hitting this dead end:
The summons your mother received
Never reached her in time to put
On an Americanized face in court
And plead her child's case.
            So, it's come to this.

The fact that you are coming to me
Speaks your desperation, a teacher
From whom you've earned straight Fs.
You politely ask me if I would please
Compose a letter that will in some way
Convince the judge who issued
Your deportation orders that
You are indeed a human being,
One who breathes, one who can
Prove his allegiance to the flag
And our cultural values by reciting
The lyrics to five Kendrick Lamar songs,
By rushing the drive-thru at least
Once a day at McDonald's,
By sporting Kenzo jeans
And the latest Affliction T's.
But I need more than your outside
Yankee-ized smile and gelled hair.
How have you done in other classes?
   Like yours.
Do you play any sports, represent
The school in any way?
   No, no social security number—
   If I get hurt, I can't see a doctor.
Well, what about a job, helping
Support your family, looking after
Younger brothers and sisters,
Anything I can say to the judge to convince
Him you will be a productive, contributing
Member of society if pardoned?
   I'm the youngest. No official job.
   My father works sixty hours
   A week at a relative's, all under

The table, so we can't say
Anything about work.
I fix cars for my friends.
I'm a good mechanic.
I assess the situation and
My potential quarry, a judge
With not one donor dime
On the line or vote in the pot,
In this age of illegal paranoia,
A lunatic constituency drunk
On xenophobic delusion.
Xhavit, I will only admit to you
Now that I lied gently for you—
Yes, I told the truth when I
Said you were a polite, respectful,
Kind-hearted young man.
I can stand by all that.
But I mentioned nothing of your grades
Or total lack of effort in my class, saying
Only that you have lived a very stressful life,
Moving often, no chance to make
Longterm friends, no driver's license,
No sense of place—fearful.
That was the poet in me, using a little
License to fill in the gaps strewn
About your pot-holed history.
I said you hoped to become a mechanical
Engineer and not just a plain mechanic,
But that's on me, not you.
I lied because I saw you willing to become
No more or less than what your American
Peers will become, another face in
Our national team picture, someone

Who will feed the quotidian need,
For a plasma screen TV, more mouths to feed
With Monsanto seeds and a dream
Tucked securely in a billfold filled with
With paper and plastic.

On Monday after class, I quietly hand you
An envelope with my letter.
You smile, thank me, shake my hand.
On Tuesday, you have dropped out of school.
I take roll and begin my lessons for the day.

—John Jeffire

Untethered

Lisa Heidle

Until I stumbled across an article about him in the paper, I never realized how much Walter Dodge and I are alike. We are both trapped in this one-horse town is the most striking similarity.

The bad economy, in tandem with the controversy spurred on by the close-minded parents at my teaching job in Chicago, forced me to seek employment at any school that would have me. I called my old boss the day I got the job and told her she was wrong—someone would touch me with a ten-foot pole. I didn't mention that it was teaching tenth-grade English to farm kids, most who've never finished a book and will never see the inside of a university. I would've said it was a step below hell if I hadn't feared her laughter.

My first spring in Stockbridge was my induction to planting season. Not a boy was present in class for six weeks. When I counted them absent, Mr. Bird, first cousin to the famous Larry Bird, a fact he shared during my interview as he pointed to a large portrait hanging above his desk of his family at a reunion, made a visit to my classroom to explain how things work in a farm community.

"We tend to look the other way during planting and harvest seasons. Their daddies need them to help out, drive the tractors and such."

"Then how do they learn the material?"

"More times than not, they don't. Just do your best to catch them up. And don't worry about including the assignments when it comes time for grade cards."

"How's that fair to the others?"

He shrugged. "Most of the other students are from farm

families. They understand and don't make a fuss. It's not really on the up and up, but you of all people should understand how that works." Mr. Bird held my gaze until I looked away. It was the first time my situation had been mentioned since the interview. I'd convinced myself it'd been forgotten.

That night on my way home, I noticed the dark earth, recently tilled, and green John Deere tractors so far out in the fields that they looked like toys. I shook my head in amazement. Kids who could barely spell their names were trusted with half a million dollar pieces of equipment and their families' livelihoods.

I pulled into the small ice cream place on the corner and ordered a burger and fries.

"Would you like a milkshake with that, Mr. Parr?" Layla Helms asked, staring up at me with the same eager look of helpfulness I'd seen her wear in class as she glanced around the room, hoping someone other than she could answer my questions on why Atticus Finch defended Tom Robinson or why Fitzgerald's anti-Semitic references were overlooked when Gatsby was published. She was the smartest student in the room, and that, coupled with a need to please, seemed to be a heavy burden for her to carry.

"That sounds good, Layla. How about a chocolate malt."

"Good choice. I'll have your order right out."

She was small, one of the smallest in the class, but had a womanliness to her. She was so innocent about her beauty that it made me ache. "Here you go, Mr. Parr," she said, sliding two white bags and my shake through the small window. "Would you mind leaving this bag on the first picnic table? It's for Walter."

"Who?"

"That guy over there." She pointed at the man across the street pacing ruts in the sidewalk. "That's Walter Dodge."

I glanced at the cloudless sky and chuckled. "Why's he wearing a raincoat?" The look on Layla's face let me know that there was no humor found in Walter's inappropriate wardrobe.

"He just does. I don't think I've ever seen him without it. This is his dinner. He won't come over until there's no one around, so just leave it."

I ate in my car and waited for Walter Dodge. Just like Layla said, he came over when the place was empty. He sat at the table, pulled a long piece of rope from a pocket in his raincoat, and wrapped it around his legs, starting at the ankles and making his way up. Once the legs were cocooned, he tied the loose end to the picnic table bench, opened his dinner and ate, looking around like a frightened alley cat. When he finished, he slowly untied the knot, uncoiled the rope, tucked it back into his pocket, and walked across the road. It was the most interesting thing I'd seen since moving to Stockbridge.

Layla came out the back door and wiped down the tables. She threw Walter's trash away and was on her way back in when I called her over.

"What's up with that guy? Is he crazy?"

"Just a little different. My mama says he's lived here all his life, but he went away for a few years to the city. When he came back, he was changed. He was the smartest person to ever go to Stockbridge High. Some people say he was beaten up when he was in the city and it made him funny in the head. Others say it was drugs."

"Why do you feed him?"

Layla laughed. "You make it sound like he's a dog or something. I don't know, I guess if it was me or someone I love, I would want someone to share a meal once in a while." Layla reached through the open window and patted me on the shoulder. "You'd do the same thing, Mr. Parr."

I nodded, relieved that I'd convinced one person of my goodness.

After the initial sighting with Walter, my curiosity was piqued. Whenever the opportunity showed itself, I would ask about him.

"I heard he killed a guy in the city and when he got out of prison, he came back here. He lives outside now, can't stand to be cooped up."

"He's like that guy from that movie. You know, he's real smart, but thinks the FBI is out to get him."

From the romantics in the bunch, I heard, "He was married in the city, but she died and it broke him in two. He hasn't been the same since." And, "His true love ran off with another guy and it made him go nuts. It happens, you know. My aunt Tilda hasn't been the same since Uncle Willard ran off with that lady who worked at the gas station."

No stories were the same, but everyone agreed on two things: Walter isn't quite right in the head and he's harmless. He's their very own Boo Radley. In all his Boo-ness, he wanders the streets dressed in a yellow slicker and green hip waders, even on the hottest days of summer. If all you see in passing is a burned dome of scalp, a permanent yarmulke, in the center of his dirty gray hair, you know it is Walter. And there's not a stronger smell in town, not even when the wind catches the pungent odor of the Burton pig farm a mile out of town. Yet everyone in Stockbridge, full of birth-born Christians who've never doubted in their shared God, treat the eyesore as if he's the second coming.

"Okay, class, I have a writing assignment for you." I waited for the moaning and complaining to quiet down before continuing. I'd spent a lot of time trying to word the assignment just right so as not to cause a stir.

"I want you to pick the strangest person in Stockbridge, then write a story about him or her. But you can't call this person by name. Write how the person became the person they are, why they do the things they do, and how you feel about that person." The laughter and chatter let me know that they would enjoy the assignment. I glanced at Layla, tucked quietly in the middle of the second row, and caught her eye. She didn't blink as she stared at me. My heart beat faster. It was a wise look wrapped in accusation.

"Do you have a question, Layla?"

"No, sir," she said, looking down.

I avoided the ice cream place for the next few days, choosing to split my meals between the pizza parlor and the small diner. I didn't want to risk running into Layla. She'd been quiet during class, and I noticed dark circles tucked beneath her accusatory eyes. After eating my lone meal one evening, I wandered the streets of Stockbridge, searching for Walter.

I found him on the steps of the old high school that sat like a dead weight in the center of town. Once the new one was built, the shortsighted folks of Stockbridge chained the doors shut and walked away. The windows were broken and grass grew up around the edges, yet there was no graffiti on the red brick. Probably because the kids fear their handwriting will be recognized, I thought to myself, taking pleasure in my wit. Considering there are only forty-seven people in this year's graduating class, my logic was probably sound.

Walter had tied himself to the rusted handrail and looked comfortable enough for a nap. I didn't do anything at first, just watched. Then I grabbed a few pebbles off the ground. Standing at the corner of the building, I tossed them in his direction.

His first reaction was to tighten the rope that kept him affixed to the handrail. What he thought that would accomplish was beyond me. The first time I hit him was an accident, but his fumbling around, trying to untie the knots, kicking his wader-covered feet, his legs flopping about like an unattractive beached mermaid, made me laugh, something I hadn't done in a while. I didn't want it to stop. I stayed until he got himself out of the rope and scurried away. I chuckled all the way back to my apartment, feeling better than I had in months.

I spent the next few days brainstorming my next move. It seemed like a lack of imagination to repeat the pebble toss, so I settled on tracking him through town. At first it was boring, but on the third night, Walter noticed me. I followed him down Logan Street, around the pool hall, and into the alley behind Fellure's grocery where he stopped to dig through the pastries that had been thrown out that morning. They were placed on top of the dumpster, double-bagged, like he'd put in the order himself. He was well into his third donut when he saw me leaning against the cold brick. The startled expression on his face made me smile. He dropped his half-eaten Long John and scurried out of the alley. I tracked him, not rushing, just at a nice meander. Walter cast quick glances back at me. I smiled at him, thrilling at his reaction.

Some would say I'm a bully. I disagree. I just have a gift for seeing the weakness in others. Like I can tell you that Casey Tillman is gay, even though he tries to hide it. I see the way he stares at Roger Cartwright all through class. When I'm tired of seeing him slump in his chair, his long legs stretched out like he's at home in his living room, a dumb, bored expression on his face, I'll make my way down the aisle, stop beside him, tap on his desk, and say, ever so quietly, "I don't think the answers are written on the back of Roger's head." The blush that spreads across his face gives me such a feeling of power, I feel like I can fly. That's the way it felt with Walter, as if I was sprouting wings.

Walter lost me near the library. I stopped at the back door and listened. The squeak of rubber on cement let me know that Walter and his waders were right around the corner. I hurried to the other side of the building and waited, heart hammering and palms sweating. I was having a hell of a time, plus getting a little exercise, something that always improves a person's disposition. Walter rounded the corner, moving faster than I'd ever seen him, his hands clenched in fists, pulled tight to his chest. I waited until he was inches from me before muttering the phrase I'd thought up the first time I saw him eating his Layla-burger, looking around like a spy on crack. "Hello, Walter. I finally found you." He was so close, I could smell his foul breath.

He opened his mouth to speak, the security light on the side of the library turning the two teeth left in his mouth blue. I waited expectantly to hear what Walter could possibly have to say to me.

"Why?" he asked.

"Why not?" was my quick response.

He stepped toward me, the fear on his face clearing and, for the first time, I felt a little afraid of the strange man who haunted the streets of Stockbridge. He reached into his pocket and withdrew the rope he used to tie himself down.

"See this?" he asked, shaking it in my face.

I nodded.

"Do you know what this is?"

"It's a rope."

"You're wrong. Look again."

I did what he asked. "It's a nasty piece of rope."

"And you're a nasty piece of man. This isn't a rope. It's a tether. It holds me here, so I don't fly away."

My mouth dry with fear, I muttered, "That's ridiculous."

"You'll understand soon enough. This town and the rest of the world are locked in a battle." He stepped into the street, then turned back to me. "I disappeared once. I didn't have the rope. Now that I have it, I won't disappear again."

I watched him walk away with what looked like a swagger in his step.

The writing assignment I gave the kids was due at the end of the week. I'd forgotten about it after my encounter with Walter and the sleepless nights that followed. No matter how hard I tried, I couldn't forget what he said. Was it the ramblings of a crazy man or was there wisdom jumbled up in his words?

Their writing wasn't half-bad, but the descriptions were so obvious, that even I, someone who'd only been in town a few months, knew who each person was within the first paragraph. Most of the class had picked one of their parents, a few chose a sibling or a classmate.

Only four people wrote about Walter, which disappointed me to no end. I'd imagined everyone in the room would have zeroed in on him—he was obviously the strangest thing in town and would make great reading. Three of the essays described him perfectly, all the way down to his waders and the slap-slap of his rubber boots as he walked down the center of the road. Two gave me new information. One was Casey Tillman. He wrote, "My uncle is a lawyer and has done some work for this guy's mom. She lives on Oak Lane. I guess he lives there, too. She takes care of him but worries about what will happen after she dies. There's no family left but her. My uncle says that she has a buttload of money, so I'm sure there's enough to pay for him to go to a crazy house when the time comes. It's important to take care of yours, my dad always says, and I think he's right."

The other was Mandy Morganstrom. She's a bit of a loudmouth who likes to deliver one-liners to make the class laugh. She'd completely missed the idea of the assignment and had stapled an old newspaper profile piece of Walter Dodge to the half-page of writing she'd done. A young Walter, all his hair and teeth intact, stared back at me. That's how I learned about how similar Walter and I are. He, too, is an only child, we both like to read and love the outdoors. And he was born in December, a Sagittarius, just like me.

Layla wrote about him, too. "There's a stranger in our midst who has slithered into town, watching the townsfolk like we are monkeys in a zoo. No one knows much about him, though everyone speculates about his past. He seems to live in a world of his own. Lack of self-awareness and judgment are his only friends. The stranger doesn't understand how a town is a living, breathing entity, full of life and story and hope. When one of us hurts, we all hurt. When one of us succeeds, it's a shared story that gets shelved as part of the combined history of Stockbridge. The stranger's smirk that he carries like a shield, directing it at everyone and everything he sees, rips a hole in my heart and makes me want to protect my little town, the only home I've ever known."

Her essay on Walter was a bit vague and sentimental. I had no choice but to give her a B.

Shadows

I draw Plato's cave on the blackboard in Humanities class,
navigating my steps through anthills of crushed chalk bits
in the process—little crack cocaine landmines, I call them.
The kids laugh. They like it when you make a drug reference.

The cave looks more like a whale, *Like that Carvel cake
whale*, Bennie says. I step back and admire the art from
a distance. *Very like a whale*, I say. "Where's that from?"
No one knows. No one cares. No one reads. For naught.

Melville quoted the line in the "Extracts" section of *Moby-
Dick*. They giggle because I said *dick*. I say it again,
this time with dramatic aplomb. *What does* aplomb *mean?*
I ask. Does anybody read? Leon wants my top-five novels

of all-time. It's a diversion. They want me to quit talking,
quit the Socratic method, quit chalk stepping. I'm in a mood,
so I take the tangent and go with it. Why not? These are but
shadow days. Shadow SAT scores, shadow desks, shadow
chairs, shadow chalk, shadow raised hands, shadow career.

—*Joseph Rathgeber*

Proctoring

Arrange the rows.
Clear the aisles.
Open a window so there's air.

Write the start time
and the end time
on the dry-erase board in bold.

Take attendance.
Distribute exams.
Give detailed instructions.

Watch the clock.
Count the students,
the floor tiles, and the scrap paper.

Figure out the ratio
of righties to lefties,
blondes to brunettes. Double-check.

Walk the aisles.
Scan for cheat sheets—
under palms, test booklets, crotches.

Announce the time
remaining. Start
collecting exams. Alphabetize them.

Dismiss the students.
Pack the materials
into the manila envelope as though

it means more
than you—or anyone else
for that matter—know it does.

—Joseph Rathgeber

Memoranda

The memo dated September nine says the budget
failed to pass. Please use the copier sparingly.

The memo dated September fourteen says paper
will be rationed. Each teacher is afforded a thousand
sheets a month. Swipe your ID card to log-in.

The memo dated September twenty-five says
teachers must submit originals to administrators
for approval. Order sheets are available in the faculty room.

The memo dated October·seven says teachers
must supply their own paper for copies. Paper
must be white, eight-by-eleven, and acid-free.

The memo dated October fifteen says teachers
are responsible for stapling their own copies.

The memo dated November three says copy orders
must be placed with administrators for review
forty-eight hours in advance. Place in bin in front office.

The memo dated November twenty says the copier
is out of order. So fuck you, faculty, and fuck
your fucking copies. Learn to be more flexible.

—Joseph Rathgeber

The Great White Way Is

Where the Heart Is

Isabella David

Sometimes, when it's quiet, I can remember what my life was like before moving to Cedar Springs. Not that it was ever quiet in New York, but there are moments when the children's voices fade away down the hall and I'm alone on stage. When I shut my eyes and breathe in the dusty air of the high school theater, I can almost taste in that sweaty air fecund with hormones and hope what it was like to be so ambitious and full of dreams again as these children all are with their starry-eyed visions of greatness.

I don't mean to sound cynical; there would be a tenderness in my tone if you could hear me telling this story aloud instead of reading what I feel compelled to write—a tenderness born out of painful experience. I have seen the light go out of so many eyes; if in any way I can help the light burn a little brighter for these kids before the world does its mad stamping act on the sparks of their tender, fiery souls then I'm happy to try to play the guru.

I even grew a beard. Still, who would have thought Tom Grantham, so full of promise, even genius some said—and those somebodies were Broadway somebodies who knew of what they spoke—that he'd end up teaching high school in a town famous for its prodigious production of red flannel and little else?

There are moments, these quiet moments, when standing up here alone in the forlorn spotlight, opening my eyes to the cracked and worn seats so many butts have wriggled and elbows squirmed in until the very vinyl is pierced innumerably that the air turns a little bitter in my mouth and it almost tastes like failure. And then the children come back, and to be surrounded by such innocence is a little like finding my own lost youth again: "The silence of pure innocence persuades when speaking fails." The words of an attendant, true. *The Winter's Tale*, Act Two, Scene II. Not the lead, not the star. . . "one that will do to swell a progress, start a scene or two." But they comfort me. I stopped speaking in the city before I left. I mean, I always *spoke*. But people stopped hearing me. I was like a ghost, all insubstantial. The silences here persuade me to hope again.

I'd go to auditions only to learn I was no longer the burning bush. That torch had passed. (Forgive the mixed metaphor; I'm only an actor, for chrissakes.) I had seen it happen to other actors, and I had thought *how sad*, but I despised not pitied them their palpable aura of failure. I had seen that torch pass to me in my early days and the chagrin on the faces, lined and patient, warning me with their tired gazes my youthly gawp might only be that—one great wild yoop before the world had its way with me and fate decided my path would take another turn away from what my promise had so clearly promised me.

But this sounds like self-pity.

I need to change the subject from past to present: I'm Tom Grantham, drama teacher at Cedar Springs High School, a father, and a husband. And I'm happy to play those roles. Honest to God I am. Of course, despite what the school's website says about the "importance of the arts in a child's development" I don't *only* play that role. I make myself "useful" and "productive"—Principal Zarsky's favorite words. I substitute, oversee the chess club, assist the hockey coach. I even built an electronic library catalog for the school when they converted from a finger-slicing card catalog to computers—our quaint, old librarian doesn't know her Macintoshes from her PCs. But now this sounds like the C.V. of sour grapes, my twin, Rachel, would say.

No, Rachel is not my identical twin. That would seem self-evident, but you'd be surprised how many people ask after finding out I have a *female* twin. We have the same black hair and eyes, but Rachel is tiny and round where I'm tall and thin. She lives in England.

Now there's Skype, and we always manage to talk a few times a week. She reconnected with some family over there, and I can say this without vanity but with the license of a twin: The only thing she misses about America is me. Besides our parents, we don't have a lot of family, unlike my wife, Julie, who seems to be related to every other person in this small, picturesque town.

One of these days, I want to get over to England and visit Rachel, but I always find an excuse not to. First, I was so busy with my "career"—God, I was a prick—and then when that fell apart, I didn't want Rachel to dub me a loser. If you had met me in that ten-month period when I lost *it*, the charisma I'd always relied on, you, too, would have dubbed me a loser.

And I was.

I began working in several bars on the Lower East Side, subsidizing my efforts to drink myself into a nightly stupor. Or a morning one, really. Bars in Manhattan stay open until four a.m. By closing time, I'd frequently greet the dawn outside the gates. Until one morning's inspiration.

"What light through yonder window breaks? It is the East and Juliet the Sun. Arise fair Sun and kill the envious Moon...."

By "envious" I was screeching, all abjuring Hamlet's best advice: I was out-Heroding Herod. I had played Romeo when I was still male ingénue material—fresh and fearless. The louder I shouted, the more I thought I'd be able to feel again.

A musician and a cop had both stopped to watch the performance. I recommended louder:

"WHO IS," *hiccup,* "ALREADY PALE AND SAD WITH GRIEF?" *Hiccup.*

The officer stepped forward with palpable menace, and then I heard the softest voice speak:

"That's my boyfriend, officer. He just lost his...cat. *Our* cat. Very attached, very sad. I'll take care of him."

She was carrying a violin case (a viola, actually, I found out later). She had the round unmade-up face of a Madonna. What New York City cop could stand before such potent innocence?

After that, she told me her name was Julie. We both took it as a good sign. At least it was the right kind of jokey story to start a love affair with. I sobered up, moved back to her hometown, and ended up working at a high school, not to mention fathering a pair of my own twins.

So, I've been busy these past few years; I know that's just an excuse for cozying up to the known world, but honestly, the whole family drama angle kind of terrifies me.

I'm happy for Rachel, though. She found her home in England, but I've found my home here with a family I made myself from the ground floor up.

Anyway, this wasn't supposed to be about me—I'm still a New York actor at heart, I guess. I love talking about myself. Jesus.

This was supposed to be about Jasmine.

In New York, we joked about the destiny of *actresses* whose own parents dubbed them Cherrys or Bambis or Jasmines. Her mother innocently explained to me at parent-teacher conference night that she named her baby after her favorite Disney princess.

Details like that make me feel my age. Her mother scarcely looked old enough to be the mother of a seventeen-year-old kid, and I had this vision of her watching a cartoon while birthing a child and then holding it like a teddy bear. The child was an unlikely Jasmine to boot: a dishwater blonde with iridescent aquamarine eyes and a round, healthy, all-American moon face. Nothing about her said exotic Arabian princess. She was the Red Flannel Festival queen runner-up her junior year. Nicole Hall-Smith was sashed or crowned queen (I don't know beauty pageant verbiage), the same Ms. Hall-Smith who was the lead in the school play the following year.

Jasmine's one of a type I saw too often in New York: desperate to shine but lacking the requisite talent, or rather ignoring her natural, God-given talents in favor of chasing that bitch-goddess Fame.

I wanted to give Jasmine the lead. That's the damnedest part of being a drama teacher. I liked Jasmine, but she couldn't remember lines to save her soul. It was nerves probably. She was a bright kid, eager to learn, which as you grow older you value more than God-given brains. How many flaccid, self-righteous prigs who are neither productive nor useful did I meet bartending who gave themselves Napoleonic airs because they'd read all of Joyce's *Ulysses*? Twice.

I knew all that about her from having her in my class throughout high school. I would have rigged the system, but then I found out she couldn't sing soprano, although she gave it her almighty best at her callback, hitting all the notes but for the key ones, and well...I tried to give her a small but integral role, and she accepted with good grace. She was a good kid; she was never voted most popular or most likely to succeed, but her name would be tossed around in the air come superlative time. She never made homecoming queen, but once she was in Nicole's court.

I know what it's like for these small-town kids when they always have to play second fiddle to the kid who's blossomed. You try to tell them their time will come, too, but that isn't strictly true and most know it. Some people's times never come. There's an element of gumption to it, and Jasmine didn't have gumption. At least when you get out in wider pools you don't have to live literally in the shadow of the big fish.

I don't know if all this was what made her so attractive as prey. I think in terms of protecting, not preying upon those weaker than myself, which is probably why I've ended up poor and middle class and lined around the eyes. Of course that's self-righteous of me, and I've indicted self-righteousness previously in the form of Joyce-thumping Ivy Leaguers. I think, like my favorite playwright Shaw, we all possess every quality. So given the right circumstances, perhaps I'd turn predator myself. But not for Jasmine Hart, never for the minnows of the world. I'll say that for myself.

I'd also like to claim in all self-righteousness that I never liked John Bradshaw, our American history teacher, but I did. It was hard to dislike John. He coached track, and he, like me, always had an open door, gathering a motley crew of misfits at lunchtime, except mine were the drama kids and his tended to be your garden-variety geeks.

Of course, I can't help thinking now what if? What if I had given Jasmine the lead in the musical, be damned the prejudices of the tune-hearing to the tune-impaired? What if Jasmine had found her lunchtime home in my classroom—that key time in a child's development where their parked seats define their souls—instead of John Bradshaw's lair? (Although I never thought of it as a lair, not until afterward.) And most important, did anyone but me suspect what happened to Jasmine Hart?

But I have no evidence, you see. I haven't got anything like proof.

The day it happened it snowed unlike anything the school district had seen. School was closing, a little known occurrence in cold Michigan, and there was mad jubilation in the halls but for Jasmine, who looked downcast. We had just had callbacks, and I had again dashed a Hart's hopes against the granite ambition of a Hall-Smith.

Perhaps that's why I followed her. I wanted to have a word with her, maybe comfort her. No, let me be honest here. It was more likely I'd scold her with that ready salve to the drama teacher's conscience: There are no small parts, only small players.

Yes, how dare Jasmine make me feel guilty! I don't think Herod upon hearing he'd nailed a god to a tree could have felt more like a destroyer of innocents. Ready with a priggish spiel for the second time in my life to out-Herod Herod, a steely glint in my eye, I approached.

Between me and Jasmine swam a sea of jubilant youths. It

wasn't until I found myself outside John's room that I realized I'd stalked her all the way down the hall, no doubt gesticulating and faintly speaking under my breath. I shook myself with the mind's eye's sense of the ridiculous.

Ready now to team up with John and buoy this young person's spirit, I raised my hand to open the door when—

"It can't happen again," a man's voice said. "It was a one-time thing. A mistake."

"But I thought you said—"

I heard the pleading in the young girl's voice.

"Excuse me, Mr. Grantham."

One of Bradshaw's geeks pushed past me into the room. The conversation changed immediately.

It was Jasmine's cheerful alto (not soprano) again: "I guess if that's your decision, Mr. Bradshaw."

"It is. Sorry, Jasmine," Mr. Bradshaw said in a hearty tone. "You're a great kid and...."

"That's all right," Jasmine said. The garden geek had widened the door enough, so I could see her face and the back of his head. She looked pale beneath her track-team tan and very still. Then Bradshaw turned away to speak to the newcomer, and Jasmine backed away several steps, her gait strangely clumsy and slow. She zipped her backpack, settling both straps on her shoulders. When she burst through the door, I wasn't able to do more than call her name.

"Jasmine," I said, uttering that ridiculous name for the last time and feeling as ridiculous saying it as I had the first. More than ever it seemed an ill-fated name.

Snow blanketed the school. When I left, all was eerily silent, and I was sick at heart.

That night, Principal Zarsky called all the teachers in the

school personally. Jasmine Hart's mother had found her hanging from her canopied bed. It was an unusual way for a girl to kill herself; girls usually poisoned themselves. Boys shot or hanged themselves. Those were my first thoughts.

But there were no words to speak what I was feeling, wondering, speculating about frankly.

"Did she leave a note?" I asked finally.

"No. Sometimes in these sudden cases . . . . The mother naturally isn't ready to do too much talking about the incident, yet, but I want to get all the teachers ready. We're going to need to be there for Jasmine's friends and acquaintances when this blizzard clears. She was popular, and incidents like this have a way of spreading. We are not going to allow that to happen under my watch. I want everyone prepared to be useful." Zarsky spoke with military menace, marshaling her troops.

"She was in my drama classes all four years."

"Really?" Zarsky said. "I didn't know that. I never saw her in any performances."

"I never cast her. Not until now, actually, this upcoming one, a silent role. She had a lot of trouble remembering lines."

"It's not your fault, Tom."

"I know that. But it doesn't mean it doesn't feel like it."

"You go talk to your wife and family now, Tom. Try to keep some perspective."

We hung up. I didn't tell her about my suspicions about Bradshaw. What proof did I have to present? Perhaps simply that he cast her when I didn't and then cast her off, when I hadn't. We both toyed with Jasmine Hart. Is his guilt really so much greater than mine?

Afterward, Bradshaw threw himself into his next role. He became more popular than ever, his door always open, his ear always tuned to the kids. I watched him, but I never caught another whiff of a similar incident. And to this day, I've never asked him about what I overheard. I can't get over a sense that I was as much to blame as he was. I can't stand to talk about it, but it's there inside me: the memory of her pale, still face, the blizzard silhouetting her in the cold fluorescent space spread like a butterfly on a cold, piece of glass.

Was she my sacrifice to my bitter old dreams? Am I just being self-indulgent?

I don't know. But like I said, this isn't really about me.

I'm all right after all. I found my home. That's all anyone needs, no matter what these kids think. It doesn't have to be glamorous; it has to be real.

Sometimes, when it's quiet, I can feel the ghosts of all the kids who've graced this stage then vanished into "the air, into thin air," year in, year out. Those who can, do; those who can't, teach. They'll find out one day, not yet, but soon, which side of the equation they'll fall under. And most of them will survive the process. I did.

A Report on My Administration
of the AP World Exam

Our experiences
are not so different.

The whole glacier melt
of human endeavor
courses down upon them,
scratching caverns
from their minds'
narrow crannies.

Their pencils,
tremoring little stalactites,
etch circles into the page.

Meanwhile, I quake
before the tsunami
swollen up before me—

four more hours
of testing to go.

I start my next lap
around the room—

the future shivers
as I approach.

—John Pierce

It Has Everything to do With Horace Walpole

Eric Appleton

Rachel's first trip to England didn't go as planned. That was obvious from the very first PowerPoint slide projected on the conference room's screen. Everyone—even Doctor Newett, known campuswide for his ability to stare *Tropic of Cancer* square in the eye and reduce Henry Miller's libido to the urgency of dry white toast—shifted uneasily in their seats, and the air pressure palpably lessened with the sudden group intake of breath. Rachel stood next to the screen, cordless mouse in hand, acting as though this was all going to be horribly, unsurprisingly academic.

Dr. Higginbotham, our department chair, tapped a fingernail on the conference table. It was the signal she was gathering her thoughts and we should all wait for the words to arrive. "That," she said finally, "that…would not appear to be a picture of anything…remotely connected with…Horace Walpole, would it?"

"It has everything to do with Horace Walpole," Rachel said.

"It *is* ten-thirty in the morning on…March twelfth, correct?"

"That's why I'm here."

"Just to be sure," Dr. Higginbotham said, "this is the report you're…giving…on your sabbatical research trip?"

"Yes."

"So…is there a connection…between what we are currently looking at and…the origins of English gothic literature?"

"When you start with Horace Walpole, this is where you may end up. It was all quite unexpected."

"He's kind of young, isn't he?" Meredith Peterson observed, prompting a sharp look from Dr. Higginbotham.

Rachel nodded. "He said he was nineteen. I decided to take him at his word."

"He's naked," Meredith blithely noted. Our chair's eyes narrowed. Consequences would follow this outburst.

"Yes. He's also a big fan of Neil Gaiman, who I might add, while contemporary, is wholly an heir to the traditions of the genre."

Dr. Higginbotham tapped her fingernail again. "You are aware, Professor Thompson, that...misuse of sabbatical funding is a...serious matter? And that as part of your first post-tenure review, this report on your sabbatical project...carries a certain amount of...weight?"

Dr. Newett cleared his throat and pointedly averted his gaze toward the window. Sex as text was one thing; being forced to acknowledge that it existed beyond the printed word was quite another. Bad enough he had to face all the sloshing, clueless hormones of the average college student in the thunderdome of the lecture hall, but here, right there, on the screen, he was being visually assaulted by a naked nineteen-year-old English lad, who sat splay-legged on a futon with sheets and blankets in a mountainous post-coital jumble around him, looking up and grinning toothily at the photographer. I suspected that it was the first time a penis—uncircumcised at that—had been so brazenly presented to the English department. The young man held a mug of tea with one hand and an open copy of Elizabeth Gaskell's *Gothic Tales* with the other. His head was shaved, and a full sleeve tattoo of twisting, gear-meshing, steampunk design wound up one arm and spilled across his chest—definitely far beyond any definition of hotness that Rachel and I had ever discussed.

Pushing back her chair, Dr. Higgenbotham clipped her pen to her moleskin notebook and rose. Dr. Newett followed suit. Professors Jones and Patel slid their chairs away from the table. As consensus had been reached, Professor Dykstra felt able to retract his ballpoint, and Dr. Buell tightened the cap on her water bottle. Meredith looked around at our colleagues. "But there's more, isn't there?" As one of the untenured faculty, she was taking a tremendous risk. During the two years she'd been in the department, it had become harder and harder to tell if her innocence masked cunning or simply deeper innocence. Was she playing chess or moving pieces around the board without rhyme or reason? If you played the village idiot, would the evil queen deign to notice you? Rachel, however, had clearly decided to upend the board and gleefully stomp the pieces into the carpet. I wanted to applaud.

Rachel raised an eyebrow. "You don't want to see the rest of my report?"

Dr. Higgenbotham looked her up and down with the glare she reserved for the naughtiest of naughty students. "Doctor Thompson...I will wait for the written version."

Rachel smiled wickedly and clicked the mouse. The slide changed. "Let me show you his ass first. It was amazing."

It was a bad day to teach *Dracula*. It was a worse day to have one of my semester's required in-class peer observations while teaching *Dracula*. I'd prayed that the morning's gothic chaos might have distracted Dr. Higginbotham from her appointed rounds, but she was nothing if not punctilious in her tyranny. Her pinched presence in the back of the room worked a vampiric spell of desiccation and ruin as I tried to avoid all mention of sex and focused instead on death, which, after all, is the other half of the equation. There are only two themes in literature, I tell my students: sex and death. And really only death when you consider that sex is an effort to leave something behind after death. Every word out of my mouth was accompanied by frenzied silent commentary and second-guessing, my attention flitting back and forth between thirty-five restive students and every brow lift, lip purse, and pen scratch my chairperson made. I was about to throw in the towel and randomly order a student to lead a discussion on a topic pulled from thin air when Jeannie Simmons raised her hand and pointed out that I had muttered something about Lucy Westenra standing in for Victorian something and then stood staring into space for a good twenty seconds. "You're not having a stroke, are you?"

Dr. Higginbotham's pen skittered across the page.

"No, Jeannie. Thanks for your concern. I was just in a, uh, interesting academic space there for a moment. Jeannie, what do *you* think Lucy symbolizes?"

"That getting bitten by a vampire is bad?"

Oh dear God.

"Why do *you* think she gets bitten by the Count?"

"Someone had to be first, right?"

"Yes, but Stoker, as the writer, gets to choose who gets bitten first. So why Lucy and not say . . . Mina?"

Ryan's hand shoots up. The pirate ship has tossed me a lifeline. "Ryan?"

"Because she's easy."

"Easy how?"

"She wants it."

If he thinks she's some sort of proto-slut, he's gonna have to say it out loud himself. "Can you point out where Stoker tells us Lucy *wants* to become one of the undead?"

"Well, I mean, if Mina's the good girl, that means Lucy has to be the bad girl, right?"

"Bad girl how? What's she done?"

"Well, she's got like three guys fighting over her."

"And that's a bad thing? You wouldn't want three women fighting over you? Does that make *you* bad?"

"It depends on what you do to get them to fight over you."

"So, what has Lucy *done*?" The pirate ship hoists anchor and sets sail. Too close to the shoal of double standards. "David. How is Lucy bad?" Silence. "Daegan. How is Lucy bad?" Nothing. "Ryan's right. Mina's the good girl and Lucy's the bad girl. But why? What has she done that Stoker kills her off? Anyone?" Visions of naked college students enjoying Gaskell's *Gothic Stories* swim through my head. He made love to Rachel on the floor of some English squat, and afterward, drank tea and *read*. And not Stephen King or *The Hunger Games* but nineteenth-century gothic tales! What heaven was that? "Okay. Fine. Who read the chapters assigned for today?"

Ryan. Jeannie. The goth girl who sits in the second to last row off to the right whose name I can never remember. Three out of thirty-five. "Really? Really?"

"Why *are* we reading it?" Connor asks. "I mean, does anyone really read this book anymore? Unless they're forced to?" Murmurs of agreement. "I mean, the movie's better."

"Which movie?"

"Any of them."

"Well, unfortunately, this is a literature class, not a film class. And . . . ."

Dr. Higginbotham is watching me. I've lost control of the class. And not just today. I've lost control of the whole semester. They don't understand why we're reading *Dracula*. They haven't a clue as to why we're reading *anything* in this class. I haven't given them a reason to think it matters. Because I assumed it was worth teaching, I assumed they would think it was worth learning. Why does it matter? Why read *Dracula*? Why care that Lucy Westenra is standing in for pushy women who want too much, who need the attention of too many men, who crave the marriage of advancement, who thinks she can get away with acting upon her base desires—or at least the base desires that rigid Victorian moral codes allow her? She *wants* to transgress—which in itself is damning enough—but isn't allowed to (gasp—what decent woman courts *three* men at the same time?), so the Count, the Count is there, he takes her across the threshold of her darkest, most forbidden desires, and for that, she must die. She must die in order to taste those desires, and then she must be destroyed because there is no way back for her.

"When you guys read the book, we can talk about the book." And for the second time in a day, I walk out of a room despite thinking it is a very bad idea.

Dr. Newett stood the requisite twenty-five feet away from the front entrance to Haier Hall, smoking his afternoon cigarette. I should have recognized his gray overcoat and fedora as I pushed the door open, but I didn't, and since he turned to see who was exiting, it was too late to turn tail and leave via a different route. Cordiality. Collegiality. The pecking order. He took a last puff and nodded as I approached; a few flakes of late snow drifted in the air, and a breeze rattled the naked hawthorns lining the walkway. Suddenly, the moment had turned very John le Carre— world-weary, vaguely sinister, presaging the exchange of clandestine information.

"Jane," he said, flicking his butt to the walk and crushing it out with a crisp twist of his highly polished wingtip.

"Dr. Newett." The cold, gray afternoon light gave a chiseled look to his features. He would have been a striking man thirty years ago. If he'd ever had a twinkle in his eye, he would have been close to irresistible.

"I hear you walked out of class today. Bravo."

"I'm sorry?"

We paused and watched a pair of students pass and enter the building. The clandestine quality of the encounter ratcheted a tick higher. He lowered his voice. "I've wanted to do that for years." He lowered his voice even more. A dark rumble on the edge of audibility. "Care to take a walk?" Was there going to be a choice? I almost expected him to take my arm as we started down the walk, leaving the sad hawthorns behind to strike out toward the equally sad and leafless maples and oaks that dotted the campus's central grassy plaza. He asked me if I knew why the paths cut across the plaza at angles, allowing you to take the shortest straight trip between the surrounding buildings. It had to be a trick question.

"It's the most logical?" I replied.

He smiled grimly and explained that when the school had become a state university in the early seventies, the architectural firm responsible for the main cluster of poorly aging concrete Brutalist structures also laid out only four paths across the square plot of grass, effectively splitting the plaza into neat quarters. There'd been an ugly fountain in the center of the crosshairs—a bunch of cubes on stilts smashed together—ringed by small concrete cubes that allowed you to sit down, but not so close to the next cube that easy conversation between sitters was possible. The fountain, cubes, and paths were ignored by the students, who insisted on wearing direct paths from building to building.

"At one point," Dr. Newett continued, as we walked toward the chemistry building, "the university even put a low fence around the perimeter, trying to encourage students toward the pavement. Unfortunately, the fence was low enough to easily hop, and even those students who entered through the designated portals then angled off across the grass. When they rebuilt the business school in the mid-nineties, funding to remodel the plaza was included. The fountain was relocated to a plot hidden by shrubbery behind the fine arts building, and the paths were laid out according to the geometry created by the users. They scattered wooden benches across the grass. Much more welcoming.

"You have no idea what an uproar this change caused, especially in the School of Architecture and Industrial Design," he said as we reached a bench on the far side. He sat facing the humanities building and patted the space next to him. "Those new to the campus see it and think, 'logical,' like you did. Why would it be otherwise? Why *should* it be otherwise?"

I sat beside him. "I trust, Dr. Newett, you did not bring me over here to admire the humanities building?"

He snorted. "Admire that monstrosity? It's like they said of the Eiffel Tower: eating at the restaurant was the only place in Paris you didn't have to actually look at it. I say we kill all the architects before we start in on the lawyers."

"You don't really mean that."

"Look at the damned thing, will you? Spend thirty years in that and of course it will destroy your soul."

"Is your soul in danger, Dr. Newett?"

He looked up, away, anywhere but my face. "I have decided it is time for redemption, Jane. I need you to be part of it."

"I'm not sure I'm the right person you need to ask for forgiveness. I don't even know what you've done."

"Redemption, not forgiveness. A last chance to correct things that I should never have allowed to slide." Onward, through the looking glass.

He smiled. Warmly. Which scared me even more. "I intend to retire in the next five to ten years. Dr. Higginbotham will outlast me. This is a problem. As you know, chairs serve terms of five years, and this is dependent on the votes of the tenured faculty and the recommendation of the dean. Dr. Higginbotham's third term as chair comes up for renewal next year." Prickles ran across my skin as I wondered if he was going to suggest I put my name forward as a candidate for chair . . . and then I remembered, with relief, that only tenured faculty could be chair. And that meant Dykstra? Rachel? Rachel was tenured.

"Rachel, of course, will not be with us next year."

"They can't—they can't just fire her. No matter how much Dr. Higginbotham disapproves of her."

There was pity in his eyes. "Jane," he said slowly. "Things don't happen to Rachel. Rachel happens to *them*." He sighed.

"That poor young man with the cup of tea probably didn't know what hit him." He let that thought sink in for a moment. "Rachel has tendered her resignation. We will be searching, once again, for a new member of the English department. How long have you been with us, Jane?"

"Three years."

"And Meredith?"

"Two."

"Dr. Buell."

"Four."

"Notice a pattern emerging?"

"We're all new."

"You are not the first wave of young faculty to have brief lives in this department."

"None of us have a chance?"

"Rachel made it to tenure because she is brilliant and politically astute. Her list of publications and presentations, her student evaluations, committee work, etcetera, etcetera, are such that even Dr. Higginbotham is unable to assail her accomplishments. How are *you* doing?"

Just enough publication to prevent me from perishing. I'd thoroughly mined the chapters of my doctoral dissertation and farmed the results out to obscure, yet juried, academic journals. I'd been on several panels at several moderate-sized conferences. I had taken revenge and redemption in the short ghost stories of Marjorie Bowen as far as it could take me; at least on this side of the Atlantic. I was currently putting together grant proposals to fund *my* first research trip to England to dig through Marjorie's personal papers and effects. Lord knows what I hoped to find, but the powers that be liked original source research. The more time that passed since my dissertation, however, the more I wondered if the world really required an expert on Marjorie Bowen. On paper, things were fine. Just barely fine. In reality: blech. In reality: *Dracula.* "How *am* I doing?"

"You work hard. You improve every year. Your student evaluations get steadily better, and I believe you do love to teach. You will, eventually, be an excellent teacher."

"Thanks."

"You will get there because you do the work. And unlike for Rachel, it *is* hard work for you." He cocked an eyebrow. "Am I wrong?"

I shook my head.

"It has been pointed out to the dean and the provost that we seem to be unable to retain faculty in our department."

"Pointed out by whom?"

"It has been pointed out."

Ah.

"I will be submitting my name to the dean as a candidate for department chair in an effort to undo some of the damage I have allowed to occur under Dr. Higginbotham's reign. I should have spoken up. I should have shown resistance. I should have encouraged our younger faculty members in experimentation and revision. I am guilty of perpetuating the status quo and damaging generations of students who ought to have passed through the department and been given a chance to love the books we love." The pity in his eyes turned inward.

"But—I'm not—I don't get to vote on this," I stammered.

"There is me. Dr. Higginbotham. Dr. Dykstra. As I said, Dr. Thompson will not be with us next year. If I have the support of the untenured faculty and adjuncts, if the provost has looked into matters, as she says she will, I believe that I can engineer a coup." As he hands me the microfilm, crosshairs develop in the center of my back.

"I would greatly appreciate your support, Jane."

"I have to think about this."

He rose to his feet, arthritic knees giving audible pops. "I would not expect otherwise." He touched the brim of his hat and walked away.

Clouds like tattered rags were pulled across the sky. The sun dimmed. Bare trees rattled. When the first office lights appeared in the humanities building, I finally got up and slowly walked to the parking lot.

Bishop's squatted on a corner a few blocks from my apartment complex. It wasn't much of a bar, but it was close, it was reasonably friendly, and the bartenders could be relied on to pour generous, no-frills drinks. Its distance from campus meant that students were few and far between, and though a number of fellow faculty lived in this neighborhood, the exterior was skeevy enough to drive away all but the visual artists who'd spent time in New York City. I also liked it because one of Marjorie Bowen's signature stories was *The Bishop of Hell.*

As Steve plunked down my neat two fingers of Canadian Club, I heard my name spoken from the end of the bar. Rachel. I turned and she lifted her beer toward me. "I wondered if you might show up."

I stayed where I was, three stools down and on the other side of the elderly Mr. Ryerson, nursing the latest in his usual long evening of drafts. I leaned back and replied around him. "Been a long day."

"I didn't realize you had a classroom observation today." She sounded as though she wasn't sure it was a slap-on-the-back laugh or an apology.

"I didn't think you were going to share pornography with the department."

"That was not porn."

"You didn't think it wouldn't have an impact on the rest of the day? For everyone?"

"I'm sorry." Actual regret? "I was thinking about my day. Not yours." Apology, then.

"Damned straight you were."

"Lemme buy you a drink."

I leaned forward and let Mr. Ryerson eclipse her. She got off her stool and came over anyway. "Of everyone in the department, you're the only one I owe an explanation."

A sip of whiskey and the burn gave me courage. "What's to explain? You wanted to go out with a bang. You did."

She looked puzzled. "Go out?"

"You resigned."

Surprise—and a little bit of panic?—flashed across her face. "Who told you *that*?"

Deadpan. "I have sources." Of course, my sources were her sources, were the only possible sources. "You hand in your resignation and you expected secrecy?"

"I expected a day at least."

"Where are you going in the fall?" Would Rachel have jumped without a net? The morning's presentation would suggest so; Dr. Newett's testimony claimed otherwise.

Rachel named a fairly prestigious New England college. I asked if she'd been offered the position before or after her sabbatical. "During," she said. She'd applied before leaving and flown back for the on-campus interview in mid-October. The offer came in November and she accepted immediately. "Before I'd even met Griff," she added, as though it helped her case.

"Griff?"

"The picture."

"Really?"

"Yeah." She slid onto the stool on my other side. "I met him my last week there. On a Samuel Johnson tour of London."

"How long were you looking?"

"For Samuel Johnson?"

"For jobs."

"You're kidding, right?"

I brought the whiskey to my lips, pacing it, drawing it out, making her work. "Come on, you can't tell me that no one else in that department isn't desperate to escape." I sipped. "That no one else has applications out." I set the glass down. "You are *not* going to tell me you like working in that department, Jane."

I had looked. The perennial hope that the grass would be greener elsewhere. For someone in the fourth year of her first full-time teaching job, I could definitely report that the grass was either dead or that the fence was too high. "It's the department I'm in. It's my responsibility to try to make it better."

"When you've been there eight years, tell me the same thing. I dare you."

"When was last time someone got tenured in that department? Before you. Name someone."

She thought for a moment. "Dykstra?"

"You're like a force of nature, Rachel. The scholarship, the students love you—everything. The rest of us mere mortals don't stand a chance if Higginbotham thinks any boat rocking might occur."

"You think I'm going to wait until Higginbotham retires?" She drained the bottom inch of her beer and signaled Steve for another and another whiskey for me. "I hung on because I knew once I made it to associate professor I could take that title with me and ask for a salary that comes closer to what I'm actually worth. My God, with the legislature the way it is, the way it has been, do you think any of us in the state system will ever see a raise that makes putting up with Higginbotham and friends worth it?" I had to give her that point. "I've done everything I can. I want to be someplace where I can make a difference. Not in ten years, and certainly not in a place where I'll have to wade through someone else's swath of destruction before I can start building anything. I don't want to burn out. I *will* burn out if I stay here."

It would be a lie if I claimed to not have considered the exact same arguments, felt that at the soonest expedient moment I, too, would cut my losses and run. Other than the job, there was nothing to tie me to the place. My ex-husband was still in Madison, Wisconsin, working as a medical systems analyst; the original plan had been to finally get my teaching on a faster track and, at some point in the not too distant future, maneuver our careers into geographical convergence. Neither of us had bargained on the hardships of a long-distance marriage. Why on earth were the vast majority of this country's colleges and universities out in the middle of nowhere where only half of the equation could have a career?

When I'd been offered this position—the first full-time position I'd ever been offered—we talked long and hard about all the options before us. I could have stayed in Madison, we *could* have had kids, I could have kept picking up adjunct work when it was available. His salary alone was certainly enough to keep up with both our student loans. But we'd agreed we weren't ready for kids. There were things we wanted to do together—just the two of us—before settling down and becoming responsible adults. But when we were apart, we found there wasn't enough to hold us together. The unspoken sentiment between us was that it might be possible to hit the reset button if I moved back. I wouldn't have failed. My career just wouldn't have...worked out. Was that so horrible? And if Rachel was doing the exact same thing that I would do in her place, why was I so incredibly pissed at her? What right did I have to be so angry, other than the fact she put Higginbotham in a rotten mood for my classroom observation? I still would have bollixed up the class without her presence. I'd blown it weeks before Griff's penis graced the screen in the conference room.

"I hate your freedom, Rachel," I finally said. I tossed back the whiskey. "Thanks for the drink. See you tomorrow."

Horror Literature: 1764 to 1910 was offered every other year. Since we both had scholarly feet in the genre, Rachel and I swapped the class back and forth; this was the second time I'd taught it. A higher freak and geek ratio would seem natural for the course, but the students insisted on flaunting stereotype by presenting as overwhelmingly normal. This semester, the goth girl who sat in the second to last row off to the right was the sole obvious representative of the fringes.

She wasn't a full-out, hardcore goth, but her clothing was either black or contained shocking neon colors to contrast with the black; her boots, whatever the weather, were tall and encrusted with buckles; and she wore her hair in a crisp, precise Bettie Page. Her makeup took the 1940s and turned it dark—the Andrews Sisters standing in as the Count's succubae. She was one of the few students in the class—hell, any of my students in any of my classes—who looked like she spent time getting dressed in the morning instead of reaching down to the floor, sniffing the nearest pair of sweatpants, and pulling them on.

The most distinctive girl in the class stood in my office doorway, and I could not remember her name. "Have a seat. What can I do for you this morning?"

Settling into my other chair, she set her backpack on the ground between her feet. It was black and bristled with rubbery spikes, a violently mutated hedgehog. Her eye caught the stack of essays on *Dr. Jekyll and Mr. Hyde* sitting on the end of my desk. "Oh, are you handing those back tomorrow? Can I get mine back now, or do I have to wait?" She plucked the top one off the stack before I could frame a bluff. Since I'd just finished grading the top one moments before her arrival, the name was fresh in my mind: Melody. *She* was Melody Kuchenreuther? Not the quiet redhead who sat in front of her? No wonder. Her appearance, her demeanor, had no connection whatsoever to her name. Kuchenreuther?

"Thanks," she said, folding it and slipping into a pocket on her bag. "I stopped by because I wanted to tell you that I thought you did the right thing yesterday."

"Walking out of class?"

She grinned. "You want to know what happened after you left?"

"Do I want to?"

"Yeah. You do."

"Shoot."

"There was a bit of silence for a moment or two. I mean, everyone was pretty surprised. I don't think anyone ever had a teacher just walk out like that before. Then Ryan got up and yelled at everyone for about five minutes about how they were fucking up his education and how he was paying for this class dammit and how dare they act like fucking slugs——"

"Fucking slugs?"

"Fucking slugs. And how dare they all ruin it for the students who actually were interested in this stuff and were actually getting something out of the class. And then he walked out. He slammed the door, too. So hard it bounced back open."

"I never thought he was all that interested in the class. It always seems like he's more interested in hearing his own opinions."

Melody shrugged. "Still means he's got a stake in it."

"What happened next?"

"I got up, called everyone retards for ruining what could have been a really fun class, and then I left, too. I think it kind of broke up after that."

"What did Dr. Higginbotham do?"

"Not sure. Seemed like she was just taking a lot of notes."

Dare I ask it? "*Is* it a fun class?"

She looked away and thought a moment. Uh-oh.

"I think you want it to be a fun class."

"I do."

No explosion. She forged ahead.

"But I'm not sure you know how to do it."

"Do you think I'm trying?"

"Yeah. I do. You're not the worst professor I've had."

Faint praise, dragging my soul down, down.

"I mean, it's just . . . I can't decide if you don't like the books themselves, or if you don't like the fact you have to teach them. I mean, it's all monsters, and sex, and death, and all this really great gruesome stuff—even if a lot of it is kinda dated—and you might as well be doing *The Grapes of Wrath* or whatever."

"*The Grapes of Wrath* is a great book."

"Yeah, but most of his other stuff is shorter and funnier. So why is that the only book of his you guys try to teach us? And Dickens. Come on. All the grumpy, serious stuff. What's wrong with *The Pickwick Papers*?"

"Is all hope lost for the class?"

"I mean, I'm enjoying the books. I hadn't actually read *Dracula* before, and it's pretty cool. And your lectures are okay. Like I said, I mean, I had Dr. Newett for freshman English. You are *so* much better than he is." She shifted uncomfortably in the chair; it's seldom a good thing to bad-mouth faculty in front of other faculty. "I just—I figured you should know what happened after you left 'cause I think Ryan raised the stakes a bit higher for tomorrow."

My Private Ryan moment. "I need to be worth it."

"I guess."

The stakes are higher. What would happen if I walked into class tomorrow, seated myself on the edge of the table, and just waited? Just picked one student and stared at them? And waited. Suspense, expectations. We're doing Dracula, so how do I work blood into that? Who can I get a blood bag from? Do I know anyone in the theatre department?

"Professor Vance?"

"Hm? What?"

"You're doing it again. Spacing out."

"If I can get something together for class tomorrow, would you be interested in helping me out? It would involve blood."

"How much blood?" she asked.

"That is something I have yet to determine. Hopefully a lot."

"You are *not* doing this just for Ryan."

"I'm doing it for me. Planned this ages ago," I lied. She knew I lied. She was okay with that. "Check your email tonight, and if we're a go, do you have time before class to get hooked up?"

"I will make time."

"Excellent. Thanks. See you tomorrow."

So why scare them? Why be scared in the first place, and what is the purpose of a scary story? The same as any story, everything I talked about the first day of class and failed to return to as the semester progressed. Play. We play so that we can learn to be humans. We read and listen to stories so that we can have the benefit of adventure and still have the reset button. When I face something scary, what should I do? What *will* I do? How do I even know what choices I have? But play only provides some of the benefits. Not all. To do that, you actually have to have the adventure yourself, and for that, play will prepare you. If there are no stakes, how do you learn things about yourself that really matter?

After Melody left, I called the theatre department office and left a message, asking if there was someone who could help me rig up an exploding blood pack for a class tomorrow. If no one got back to me, there was still the Internet. Even if I ended up duct taping a baggie full of ketchup to Melody it would still be worth it.

I opened a new document and typed:

Assignment: Due, Wednesday, April 4. Tell me a story. No, tell me two stories. Tell me two chilling tales of horror and suspense. Here are the rules:

Story #1: Good must win in the end. It need not be a neat victory. Someone must learn a lesson, or a relationship must be restored. A supernatural entity must play a pivotal plot role.

Story #2: Despite everything, the hero/heroine goes down. No lessons are learned, except, perhaps, that nothing you do will make a difference. A supernatural entity is the antagonist.

Make them scary enough that I sincerely fear for the hero or heroine but hope they can make it.

Gore and sex cannot be gratuitous, unless it's really really good gore and/or sex.

Each story, no longer than five minutes. You will tell them to the class in a darkened room with no props other than a flashlight held below your chin.

Save. It was a start.

I logged on to a travel site and bought a plane ticket for the day after grades were due. London. So much for the checking account. Hell, so much for the savings account.

Thank God I'd been to Canada for a conference last year and gotten my passport renewed. All the necessary preparation needed to be spontaneous.

The plan was that there would be no plan. If my first trip to England didn't go according to plan, I did not plan on coming back.

Fast Classroom Exit

Professors are indestructible
Stain-resistant
And laminated
We endure, but all have
A chink in our armor

I can handle the odd
And the mis-fitting
The tardy because the car broke down
And the terrified of returning to school
The early, front-row I-need-an-A-ers
And the off-target rambling storytellers
The methodical, insatiable pencil-sharpeners
And the constant-questioners who never sit still
The I-am-going-to-eat-this-hoagie-from-Sheetz-instead-of-taking-
notes-ers
And the cell phone addicts who text in their crotches

But pink eye gets me
Every
Single
Time

Out, I say
Out
Talk to no one
Touch nothing
Do not hand in a paper
Go home
Put your sunglasses on
I'm bleaching the door

Get out
And only return when
Not a trace of red
Can be found in your eyes.

—*Sarah Bigham*

The Classroom

I talk about peace, love, and understanding with the college students
taking classes between work shifts and day care
and paying the rent.

They teach me what resting bitch face means
and what it looks like
and how to accurately use phrases from current songs.

I talk about Civil Rights,
respecting our neighbors, and how
we all deserve kindness and a chance to participate.

They teach me how to dare to dream for a better future
even though nothing so far in their lives has made such an outcome
ever seem possible.

I talk with them about landlines, the satisfaction
of seeing newsprint on your fingertips, and how time seems to fly
so say it now, whatever words are in your heart.

They teach me about persistence and character and how to put one foot
in front of the other despite dead babies or abusive parents, or
traumatic times in war zones or ERs.

I am middle-aged
and we are all
getting schooled.

—*Sarah Bigham*

BE Not I

Michael Neal Morris

They walked rapidly. She was heading off campus, and he was no hurry to get to his office hour but wanted to keep up with her.

"Dentist appointment," she said. "No big deal but I don't want to be late."

"I guess I should prepare for the department meeting at two," he said. "Like it will make any difference if Professor Robb shows up."

"Better you than me," she said with a nervous chuckle.

He asked, "You won't be back in time? Guess it isn't just a checkup."

She put a hand on his elbow and stopped them both up short. They were at the end of a hallway, each office in opposite directions. They had stood there hundreds of times. Students rushed past, as they always did, just a couple minutes late to class. The same indistinct conversations rattled around them. Here they typically paused, ended the conversation, and parted.

But she was not a person who "touched." They had been colleagues for seven years, and during most of that as close as friends one could be in the environment. They had drunk together, served on committees together, and even worked out twice a week on adjoining treadmills. When his dog died, she offered an uncomfortable hug, but other than the occasional high five, their skin never met.

"No. It is just a checkup," she said. "But I'm done with committees."

He let out a combination of a snort and a giggle, a sniggle, she used to call it. "Good luck with that."

She turned to him and pulled his elbow to defeat the sidelong glance he was giving her. "I got a job offer over the break. I'm taking it." She tried to say it in her usual flat tone, but a slight tremble betrayed her.

It would take some time before he would quit torturing himself over the meaning of that rare quiver in her voice. He knew she wasn't happy there, constantly worrying about how to get by on the pittance of a salary, as one worked sixty to eighty hours a week just to keep up for post adolescents who didn't want to leave high school. Parents she loathed and friends outside of education constantly reminded her that greater rewards were out there in the corporate world.

"Three times the salary. Travel," she was saying. "No working weekends, except when traveling, of course."

"Of course," he repeated.

He didn't believe in fate, but days later he would say she was meant for the classroom.

That conversation would be over a few beers at an impromptu celebration, the last time he would see her. But in that moment, he sucked in his sorrow and feigned happiness.

"And this company—these people—have already gone to great lengths to show they want me. They flew me to Chicago. Chicago for Pete's sake, just to meet the CEO and have lunch."

And that last part, he knew, was it. He wanted her, but things like that are not said, not so much for the sake of morality as survival. He tried to push out of his head the images of all the working lunches they had had: heating up leftovers and brainstorming strategies in the department office break room, burgers and beers after one of them had dealt with a challenging student or odious co-worker, and salad bars to postmortem performance reviews.

"Wonderful," he said. "That's really wonderful. You deserve this."

"Thanks," she told him. They didn't look at each other, suddenly noticing the space was empty of students and faculty. He noticed, in the corner of his eye, a janitor emptying the trash receptacle a few feet away. Then with a quick release of his arm, she said, "Gotta go. Chat later?"

He nodded. Turning the opposite direction of her receding, liquid body, he started walking, and as he passed the janitor, hoped he didn't look like a lost dog.

Not By Arguments

Tony Press

Title taken from the 10th stanza of Walt Whitman's "Song of the Open Road."
(I and mine do not convince by arguments, similes, rhymes,
We convince by our presence.)

Judith's grandmother was dying. She had been moved from a rest home she hated to a hospital she couldn't recognize. Heredity, plus ailments, plus time, each was enough, and together claimed complete authority. Judith, four hundred miles to the north, understood the reality by day but nights were endless discomfort. She hesitated to accept the touch, the gentle words, even the breath of her beloved Mayra, knowing that with closed eyes the sorrow returned.

Judith's father had died when she was sixteen. An energetic trail-walker and thrice-a-week jogger, he fell just before his fortieth birthday. She had been sitting at the old kitchen table doing homework for Mr. Alexander as the stereo played a bouncy Sheryl Crow tune. Dad was working his normal second-shift at the docks in Long Beach. He left their apartment at 2:45 in the afternoon as, two miles away, Judith's school ended for most of the students, at the bridge between sixth and seventh periods. Seventh was optional, an opening for over-achievers like Judith, for whom high school was a feast of opportunities. She had long stopped wondering why the majority chose the opposite approach. She concentrated on what she did know: she would make it to college, and she would become a teacher, like Mr. Alexander, like Mrs. Amaya, like Ms. Anding.

She would be the next Mr. Alexander. She loved his challenges, that his every assignment was difficult, that his comments on her writing were honest, that his encouragement was unceasing. She had him twice this year: third period for College Prep English and seventh, with only four others, for "Enhanced." It wasn't quite Advanced

Placement, Mr. Alexander lamented, because the school hadn't done what it needed to do to get it approved. But, he said, if they—"the mighty five"—gave their all, he would, too, and when they were in college they'd be as prepared as anyone, official AP credits or not.

She was scribbling questions in the margins of three Thomas Hardy poems when the phone rang. Looking at the yellow clock above the sink, the clock they'd had in every kitchen she could remember, she saw it was already seven. She smiled, put down her pen, and reached for the wall phone. He often called on his lunch break. Some nights, he would receive "voluntary" overtime, an extra two to four hours. If that happened, they could go three days without seeing each other. The call served as a check-in and, just in case, a chance to say good night. When he was a teenager, he had quit school, lied about his age, and joined the army, all on his sixteenth birthday. He loved to ask her about her books. He loved an expression he'd learned from some British friends, "gobsmacked," and often used it to describe his wonder at her skills.

It wasn't her dad. It was a Doctor Rumney, asking to speak to Mrs. Richard McMahon. Judith's mother was a faint childhood scar, someone who had deserted husband and her then-four-year-old daughter. Six years later, three months after it had happened, daughter and father learned that the body of the one-time Mrs. Richard McMahon had been found in a Motel 6 in Las Cruces, New Mexico. There had been no sign of foul play. Judith said to the doctor "this is she" and was told her father had collapsed and died at twenty minutes after six.

Her grandmother was dying. Her father's mother. She had

no brothers, sisters, aunts, uncles. She had married in the middle of her senior year at Berkeley. He was passionate, driven, intelligent, terrified, and full of anger. She had matched him trait for trait. The union endured only two years, mercifully arrested by his infidelity with a co-worker. It had never been violent, though only she knew how close she had once come, while glaring at his smug face, to smacking it. And now, remarkably, she was enjoying Mayra's love and companionship. Frequently, over the past four years, Mayra had urged her to admit that Vic's cheating was a gift to all three of them, but she wasn't buying. She wasn't yet willing to give up the memory of the pain.

Last weekend, the last weekend of August, when all other teachers in California were setting up classrooms, preparing and revising lesson plans, pouring money into off-site copy machines, she had driven the four hundred and twelve miles to Long Beach to see her grandmother. The doctor said it would be a few days, possibly as much as a week or ten days, but likely no more than that. For most of the visit, she sat beside the bed, clutching her grandmother's hands and peering into the stricken and silent face. She couldn't see if her grandmother knew she was there. She chose not to ask the nurses.

After that, after getting home at three-thirty Monday morning, the first day of classes was a stunningly incoherent blur. She rode the waves of student energy and did her best not to wipe out. On her desk, not yet framed and not likely to be hung, was the Special Recognition Award she and the school had received in the summer, honoring the extraordinary success of her last year's Advanced Placement class.

At a workshop two summers ago she had re-connected with Mr. Alexander. What she hadn't understood in high school was that neither the administration nor his fellow teachers had been happy about the seventh-period class. Administration either couldn't or wouldn't pay him, and to his colleagues, working for free set a terrible precedent. Ironically—"as we know, a favorite word for English teachers," he half-laughed—he had been the campus's union representative three times. He had explained to everyone, he told her, that sometimes "you just give what you can," and "the rest will just have to take care of itself." He had remained an active union member but did not offer himself again for the representative's role. "I don't think I would have been elected," he smiled.

If there were no disturbing phone call during the week, she would get coverage for her Friday afternoon classes and coax another pair of trips from her ancient Datsun. The engine wouldn't like it, but hell, neither did she. On Wednesday afternoon, she filed the "green sheet" with the principal's secretary to request a substitute, writing "impending family death" in the box next to "reason for absence."

Thursday afternoon, as she was leaving her classroom, she found Mr. Bartlett in the doorway. Remarkably, he was walking into her room. On purpose. Bartlett, who had been at the school twenty-six years, grudgingly teaching English only to support his true calling: baseball. Bartlett, who was never, ever, without his baseball cap. Bartlett, who consistently introduced himself to new teachers, loudly, as "the old fart." He endlessly praised the days when he could smoke in his classroom "instead of sneaking off campus like some piss-ant freshman." When she had started, burning with beginner's zeal and keen to develop an Advanced Placement program at this school, a school even worse demographically and every other way than her own alma mater, Bartlett had snorted: "Kid, AP is for other schools. If they learn ABC here, we're happy."

That was six years ago, and she still avoided him as much as possible. He had exactly one virtue: his name reminded her of the Buddhist Center she and Vic had briefly attended, on Bartlett Street in San Francisco. That had been one good thing they had done together. When she had time, she might go back. She and Mayra had moved to an apartment in the outer Mission, so the center wasn't far away. When she had time. When she had space.

Perfect, just what I need. What could Bartlett want now?

"Hold on a second, kid." *He still doesn't know my first name.*

He grabbed her elbow (*Has he ever touched me?*) and forced something into her hand.

"Here's a *United* ticket to LAX. It's the 1:40, Friday afternoon."

Judith stared at the flimsy blue and red envelope, then at Bartlett. Her lips and tongue refused to cooperate. The phrase "words failed her" finally made sense.

"Take all the time you need, it's an open return. I'll make sure people cover your classes. And for Christ's sake, don't worry about your precious AP, I won't go near it. All your subs will be real English teachers, I promise."

"But, but, it's too much, it must be so expensive. No. I can drive. I was planning to drive. Why would you do this?"

"You give what you can, kid. Take the goddamn plane."

She sensed rather than saw him leave her room. Maybe he was going toward his own room, perhaps the ball fields. She held the envelope in one hand and dialed Mayra with the other. If she told her, then it would have to be real: the awe, the good fortune, the love she felt for Mayra, for her grandmother, and for Bartlett and all the rest.

In Bloom

Allie Marini

"There are a few things you need to know before we start." He writes his name, Prof. Jack Miller, on the dry-erase board. There is a stack of stapled syllabi circulating the rows of the classroom, with weekly reading schedules, due dates, online access codes, and a breakdown of how their work will be evaluated for the semester. "One of those things is that I care less about *what* you write than *how* it's written—if you're not great at grammar or punctuation, it'll count, because the Good Lord has blessed us with spell-check, but not as much as it might count in another class. I'm guessing, since you're all starting in the master's program, that your writing is what got you here in the first place. The technical stuff matters, but those are easy enough edits to make. What I care about is the how of it, the feel of it, the sound and vision, to quote David Bowie."

The class murmurs in approval and thinks of *Labyrinth*, *Ziggy Stardust*, *Scary Monsters*, or *Station to Station*. No one thinks of Tin Machine. They flip through the syllabus. Some take notes, some have their laptops open and are filling in the spaces on their Google Doc calendars so that deadlines don't sneak up on them.

"So, to begin with, I'm going to be holding you to a different kind of standard. Not necessarily a higher standard; just a different one. You all want to be writers—that's why you're here. You want to tell stories, or maybe you want to write poems—you want to put letters into structures that make words, that make sentences, that create people, that remember places, that imagine events, that represent something powerful and real to the eyes and hearts and brains that pick up your stacks of language and translate them into meaning. Since you're all in this class, in this program, I know that you're already off to a good start and that there's probably some of you that I won't really be teaching much to—there are probably a few of you that I'm just going to point in the right direction and say, *run*, to. And you guys—maybe you know which ones you are—you guys, I'm going to hold to an even *higher* standard than everybody else. Not with your writing so much, because that's something you're going to do no matter what, because you can't stop doing it, even if you wanted to. Where I'm going to make you really work is in the workshops with the writers who aren't as good as you are—yet—you're going to have to figure out how to be tough, but stay kind; how to be gentle when you guide, and how to look at someone else's work and see what it *can* be, not just what it *is now*. You are going to be helping me teach what goes and what stays, how a good image becomes great, how to get rid of the weak words without killing the confidence of the person who wrote them, how to take the paragraphs that are strong and build them into *giants*. You've already got those tools, and I'm going to make you share them—because as you all know, writing can be solitary and greedy and competitive. Look around the class—you see those faces? *They're like you.* They're *just* like you. Those people aren't your competition. They're your peers. There's room for you all to write. The ones that aren't as good as you are—you don't make them question their talent, because guess what? There's someone in here that's *better* than you, too—and *they're* going to challenge *you* to be better, just because they're here. You are all going to have to rise to the occasion in this class. You're going to have to know when it's okay to be confident and cocky and to shrug off what criticism you get. You're also going to have to learn when to be humble, when to see that your piece didn't hit its mark the way you wanted it to, and when to take those comments and suggestions and say thank you and be glad that a class of your peers wants your writing to succeed. You're going to be jealous of the stories you didn't write but should have; you're going to decide that the best thing you ever wrote is crap, and someone else in here is going to be envious that *they* didn't write it. You're going to get angry. You're going to get self-righteous. You're going to cry and question yourself—but *not* because of what your peers say. I'm going to promise you that. Criticism that isn't constructive isn't going to be tolerated here. The reason you're going to feel all those things, the reason you're going to be mad and frustrated and unsteady and miserable—that's going to be because of something *you already know*. You're a writer. You don't experience the world the same way as people who don't write, the same way that I'll bet most of you feel when you talk to someone who's in math or science. You're different. It's why you write. I want you to leave this class faster, stronger, and better than you thought you could ever be, with a list of people who you can talk to, who'll help you for the rest of your writing life, whether it's just until the program ends or whether it's up until the day they put you in the ground. *That's* the thing that you need to know before we begin. If you don't think you're ready for it, you can leave now and drop this class, or sign up for another section of it with someone else. I won't think less of you for it, either. If you're here, I want you to *be here*. Now's your chance to decide. We'll break for a few minutes so you can think about it, or get your things together, or run down to the breakroom and refill your coffee, or go out and suck down a ciggie. Your choice. If you're in, be back here in fifteen minutes. If not: that's okay, too—you'll be just fine."

Outside, the smokers cluster together, their bad habit an icebreaker between them as they nervously weigh everything Prof. Miller—or Jack, as the ones who stay will end up calling him—said and decide whether or not they're ready. The air outside smells sweet, even through their plumes of smoke, and it hasn't quite gotten warm enough for them to lose their winter jackets or scarves, but it's warm enough to leave the gloves and mittens behind. In the downstairs breakroom, a student refills his travel mug and wonders if this time it'll be any different. When he returns to the class, he doodles on the empty stretch of yellow lines gridded across his legal pad as most of the class trickles back in. Jack is reclining in the chair behind a long table at the front of the classroom as the ones who stay return one by one, some smelling of smoke and spring, others with full mugs of coffee or bags of overpriced cookies from the vending machine. He scans and counts, jots down a note that he's missing six. One comes back late, apologizing for herself as the metal door slams noisily behind her. Her stylish swing bob cups the side of her jaw as she sits down and unknots her scarf, retrieving a Pilot pen from the depths of a backpack that's clearly seen better days, and notices that the boy sitting next to her smells strangely and faintly of both curry and something bitter.

"Now, if you're ready, we'll start. I'm going to break you down into six groups to workshop. These are going to be your best friends and worst enemies for the next five months. Learn their names and put their numbers in your phone. If we need to switch any of you around, let me know by the end of the week and we can do that, but by next Tuesday these groups are going to be set in stone, so make sure you use this time to figure out if you're a night owl in a group of early birds or vice versa, because that's going to matter."

He calls out their names and they divide, like cells in mitosis of the buds on winter branches. They will uncurl into leaves, bask in the sunlight; they will wither and hibernate; they will fall and mulch themselves into compost to feed new forms. They will write and edit themselves, letter by letter, word by line, sentence by stanza, paragraph by page, poem by book, filling volumes and chapters—some will be published, still more will not—because just as surely as they have chosen words, words have also chosen them. They change their seating arrangement into the pods he has grouped them into. They are all ready to begin.

Darwin's Nightmare

The students understand trickle-down economics.
What poses the most challenge is the actual living
out of ideas of fairness, justice, the sharing of power,
or doing something with love. They do not know
how to take themselves out of the picture and
see from the perspective of the other, especially
when it is different.

We quarrel about what is right. How it differs from the
wrong. They hardly ask for explanation. They want to
make a point and have others follow it. Have me follow
it. I remind them that I am the teacher. That they need
to respect me as I respect them. That I care for them.
I see the good in them. I say these things and think
why can't they see these things in me?

On the ride home, I think of the oppressed making
excuses for the oppressors. *Nobody in the world,*
nobody in history, has ever gotten their freedom
by appealing to the moral sense of the people
who are oppressing them, says Assata Shakur.
I snap out of it. Focus on the road. I leave school
behind when I enter the door and see my daughter's
eyes. Her smile. She sees me.

In the morning, on the drive to work, I pray for
strength to survive another day.

—*Elvis Alves*

Contributors

Elvis Alves is the author of the poetry collection *Bitter Melon* (2013) and the chapbook *Ota Benga* (2017). His latest book is *I AM No Battlefield But A Forest Of Trees Growing* (2018), winner of the Jacopone da Todi poetry book prize. Elvis lives in New York City with his family.

Eric Appleton is an associate professor in the Theatre/Dance Department at the University of Wisconsin-Whitewater. Four of his short stories (including this one) have appeared in various issues of *The First Line*. He is co-author of *Teaching Introduction to Theatrical Design*, and his play for young audiences, *Three Excellent Cows*, is published by Heuer.

Sarah Bigham teaches, writes, and paints in Maryland where she lives with her kind chemist wife, three independent cats, and an unwieldy herb garden. Her work appears in a variety of great places for readers, writers, and listeners. Find her at www.sgbigham.com.

Poet and teacher **Victoria Crawford** celebrates the beauty in our daily lives and our world, but school violence, student by student, was a working condition too hard to cope with so she turned to poetry. She hopes it will help people to work for better conditions at school and on the street for all. Her poems have appeared in journals such as Califragile, Postcard Poems and Prose, Poetry Pacific, and *Time of Singing*.

Isabella David is a poet, writer, a former professional actor, and a current amateur musician. *The Voices of Women*, her first chapbook, was shortlisted for the International Venture Award and published by Finishing Line Press in 2016. She lives in Philadelphia with her husband, a trumpeter and the other half of their jazz-folk duo, and an ever-expanding menagerie of animals and children. More of her work can be found at www.isabelladavid.com or @IsabellaMDavid.

John Davis is the author of *Gigs* (Sol Books) and *The Reservist* (Pudding House). His work has appeared recently in DMQ Review, *Iron Horse Literary Review*, and *Rio Grande Review*. Having taught high school for forty years, he has recently retired.

Sheryl Guterl, a retired elementary school teacher and counselor from New Jersey, now lives in Albuquerque, New Mexico. Her poetry has been published in *The Teacher's Voice*; Months to Years; *Survival*, a poets speak anthology; and the New Mexico State Poetry Society Poet's Picnic haiku collection. Her experiences as a teacher, counselor, mother, grandmother, and traveler inform her writing.

Lisa Heidle writes flash, short-, and long-form fiction, articles, essays, and book reviews. Her work has appeared in the *Chattahoochee Review*, *Sabal LitMag*, Second Hand Stories (podcast), *Flash Fiction Magazine Anthology*, and other literary journals. Her short story collection, *én•nēad*, was released in 2017.

Matthew E. Henry is a Pushcart-nominated poet with works appearing or forthcoming in *The Anglican Theological Review*, *Poetry East*, The Ekphrastic Review, Kweli Journal, Longleaf Review, Radical Teacher, and 3Elements Review. He is a high school English teacher who received his MFA from Seattle Pacific University, yet continued to spend money he didn't have pursuing an MA in theology and a PhD in education.

A.J. Howells is the publisher and general editor of Makeshift Press, where he recently reprinted Fredric Brown's *The Office*. His prose has now appeared in two volumes of *Workers Write!*, *The First Line*, and *South 85 Journal*. His poetry has been featured in *Eunoia Review* and *The Offbeat*. RhetAskew will soon publish his novella *Alley Bats*. In his spare time, he teaches full time. He lives in the woods of northern Virginia with his wife, two children, and two cats.

John Jeffire was born in Detroit. In 2005, his novel *Motown Burning* was named Grand Prize Winner in the Mount Arrowsmith Novel Competition and in 2007 it won a Gold Medal for Regional Fiction in the Independent Publishing Awards. In 2009, Andra Milacca included *Motown Burning* in her list of "Six Savory Novels Set in Detroit" along with works by Elmore Leonard, Joyce Carol Oates, and Jeffrey Eugenides. His first book of poetry, *Stone + Fist + Brick + Bone*, was nominated for a Michigan Notable Book Award in 2009. His most recent book, *Shoveling Snow in a Snowstorm*, a poetry chapbook, was published by Finishing Line Press in 2016. For more, visit writeondetroit.com.

Allie Marini is a cross-genre Southern writer. In addition to her work on the page, Allie was a 2017 Oakland Poetry Slam team member and writes poetry, fiction, and essays, performing in the Bay Area, where, as a native Floridian, she is always cold. Find her online at www.alliemarini.com or @kiddeternity.

Barb Miller is the chairman of the Saddlebrooke Ranch Writing for Publication, and her short stories for the past four years have been place-winners in the Annual National *Writer's Digest* Competition. Barb was a teacher for thirty years.

Michael Neal Morris lives with his family just outside the Dallas area and teaches composition and creative writing at Eastfield College. His most recent books are *Release* and *Haiku, Etc.* His writing regularly appears at Two Cents On (twocentson.net/author/bluemonk) and his Tumblr page This Blue Monk (bluemonkwrites.tumblr.com).

John Pierce is a tenth-year teacher from Mason, Texas. He finds his motivation to write from the piles of essays laying around his classroom, which he should be grading. Some of his more recent writing has appeared in *Religion and the Arts*, *b/w coasts*, and Valley Voices.

Tony Press tries to pay attention. *Crossing the Lines*, his 2016 story collection (Big Table) is available in libraries and bookstores, from that Amazon place, or directly from him. He claims two Pushcart nominations, twenty-five criminal trials, and twelve years in a single high school classroom. He loves Oaxaca in Mexico, Bristol in England, and Brisbane in California.

Julie Pullman has been teaching high school English for fourteen years and working on poetry and short stories in whatever spare time a teacher and mother of two can wrangle. Her writing has placed as a finalist in the Sybil's Scriptorium DragonComet short story contest.

Joseph Rathgeber is an author, poet, high school English teacher, and adjunct professor from New Jersey. His story collection is *The Abridged Autobiography of Yousef R. and Other Stories* (ELJ Publications, 2014), his work of hybrid poetry is *MJ* (Another New Calligraphy, 2015), and his forthcoming novel is *Mixedbloods* (Fomite, 2019). He is a recipient of a 2014 New Jersey State Council on the Arts Fellowship (Poetry) and a 2016 National Endowment for the Arts Creative Writing Fellowship (Prose).

Linda Sánchez is a writer, entrepreneur, and mom to two small brown dogs. She lives in Northern Massachusetts, quite often in a state of bliss.

Joe Sottile is a former teacher, children's author, poet, performer, and essayist. He has been published in *Teachers of Vision, Once Upon a Time* magazine, *Learning* magazine, the *English Journal, Woman's World, Chicken Soup for the Child's Soul,* and in several anthologies. He was a poetry enrichment instructor for Boards of Cooperative Educational Services (BOCES), and he doesn't truly feel alive unless he is doing workshops or performing poetry for kids.

Miriam Thor received her bachelor's degree from Gardner-Webb University in American Sign Language and elementary education. Currently, she resides in North Carolina and is employed as an interpreter at a middle school. While her story is fictional, she drew heavily from her own experiences. Her previous publication credits include two novellas entitled *Wish Granted* and *Her First Noel,* short stories in Youth Imagination and TWJ Magazine, novellas soon to be published by Anaiah Press and World Castle Publishing, and a poem in Embers Igniting.